Fourth Year Triumphs at TREBIZON

Read all the titles in the
TREBIZON series

Fourth Year Triumphs at TREBIZON

ANNE DIGBY

EGMONT

EGMONT

We bring stories to life

Fourth Year Triumphs at Trebizon
First published in Great Britain 1985
by Granada Publishing Ltd
This edition published 2017 by Egmont UK Limited
The Yellow Building, 1 Nicholas Road, London W11 4AN

ISBN 978 1 4052 8072 3

www.egmont.co.uk

A CIP catalogue record for this title is available from the British Library

62832/1

Typeset in Goudy Old Style by Avon DataSet Ltd, Bidford on Avon, Warwickshire
Printed and bound in Great Britain by CPI Group

Stay safe online. Any website addresses listed in this book are correct
at the time of going to print. However, Egmont is not responsible
for content hosted by third parties.

Please be aware that online content can be subject to change and
websites can contain content that is unsuitable for children.
We advise that all children are supervised when using the internet.

MIX
Paper
FSC FSC® C018306

CONTENTS

For Connie

ONE
Back to School

'Nearly back!' thought Rebecca Mason as the taxi took her along the top road that overlooked Trebizon Bay. She gazed across the palely glinting sea to the little island that lay just offshore. It was green and newly washed-looking after a heavy April shower. 'Mulberry Island!' she thought idly, then smiled to herself. 'I'd love to row across there and explore the ruined cottage. We always say we'll do that in the summer term. I wonder if we will?'

She snuggled back comfortably as the cab approached the imposing wrought-iron gates of Trebizon School and slowed down to turn in.

'I wonder what's going to happen this term?'

Some very dramatic things were going to happen. They would never have happened if Sue Murdoch

1

hadn't been introduced to Justin Thomas in the Easter holidays. Rebecca had been there when they met (because it was Robbie Anderson who had introduced them) but since then had never given it a second thought and had no inkling of what it was all going to lead to.

She was just wondering about the coming term in a very general way. And now, as the taxi crawled slowly through the acres of parkland in which the school was set and the main building – once an eighteenth-century manor house – came in sight, she became reflective.

One thing that was *definitely* going to happen was that her parents were coming to the school to meet the Principal, though admittedly that wouldn't be until the end of term. They would be travelling along this very drive and gazing at that beautiful building in the distance, just as she was doing now. Coming down to stay, so they could talk about her future, with Miss Welbeck! Their most recent letter, written as usual on airmail paper, was in Rebecca's luggage somewhere.

We've been summonsed! it said. *Miss Welbeck wants to see us at the end of the summer term, as soon as we get back from Saudi for our annual leave. She thinks it's high time we met her and had a proper talk about your future prospects, Becky. After all, we're only home once a year – and she says you'll be taking your mocks next January.*

Apart from the mention of 'mocks', which sent a very slight tremor down Rebecca's spine, quickly banished, the prospect seemed quite pleasurable. It would be nice to have Mum and Dad come to the school for 'consultations'. That phrase 'future prospects' seemed to hold faint promise, somehow. Better make sure she did some work this term. Mustn't let tennis take over her life completely, even though everything to do with tennis seemed to be getting better and better at the moment ... It was all rather heady and exciting, the tennis.

Her friends thought so, too! As the taxi arrived at Court House three of them rushed out to meet her –

'Congratulations, Rebecca!' exclaimed Sally Elphinstone.

'You got as far as the quarter-finals then?' said Margot Lawrence. 'Tish told us the news. Didn't you do well?'

'Clever Rebecca!' Mara Leonodis clapped her hands and laughed, brown eyes glowing. 'You did *so* well at Edgbaston and now you will be selected to

3

go to Eastbourne in August, just you wait and see. Rebecca! You have four tennis rackets now – *four*. And they are all new!'

'I got them free!' laughed Rebecca. 'Here, can you lot help me carry all this stuff? I got them free as long as I don't play with any other make when I go to tournaments. That's easy because they're my favourite racket anyway!'

'I bet you and Joss Vining will be picked as first pair for the school tennis team this term,' said Elf enthusiastically. 'Two Fourth Years being the school's top tennis players, think of it!'

'And then you will go to Eastbourne,' repeated Mara rapturously. 'I shall ask Father to have me flown back to England in August to watch you! You and Joss together, both at Eastbourne.'

The British Junior Grasscourt Championships!

Rebecca laughed and shook her head so vigorously that her fair hair flew in front of her eyes.

'Hang *on*, Mara! Joss will be there I'm sure, but don't count on me making it. My ranking's not high enough – not at the moment, anyway.'

She paid the taxi driver and as the vehicle scrunched away over the gravelled forecourt, the four girls started to sort through the pile of luggage and share it out between them. Changing the subject, Rebecca said:

'Hey, how about Tish, then, scoring all those goals in Holland?'

Although she hadn't seen any sign of them yet, Tish Anderson and Sue Murdoch were Rebecca's two closest friends at Trebizon.

'She's taken some great photos –' began Margot.

'Rebeck!'

With a loud yell of delight a tracksuited figure with short dark curly hair came bounding across the grass, grinning at her.

'Tish!' said Rebecca, with pleasure.

'I was out jogging when I saw your taxi go past!'

'Good. You're just in time to help me get all my stuff upstairs.'

All chattering at once, jostling together, loaded up with Rebecca's luggage, they made for the big front entrance porch of Court House. There were two suitcases, a sports bag, three carrier bags and the four tennis rackets.

'Why did you take all this stuff home?' laughed Tish. 'You could have left some of it at school.'

'Well Robbie took me up to Gran's in the car, didn't he?' said Rebecca. 'I forgot I'd be coming back by coach. It's been an awful journey – lucky the drivers are so nice.'

Suddenly there was a squeal of brakes behind them and a very luxurious-looking maroon saloon car drew up. A uniformed chauffeur got out and came round to open the rear passenger door. Out stepped Margaret Exton, a Fifth Year girl in Court House. Rebecca caught a glimpse of a man, still seated in the back passenger seat, who called out from the shadowy interior:

'Take me over to the main building now, Baxter, or I'll be late for my appointment. You can leave Margaret's luggage till later.'

'Very good, sir.'

The five friends stood watching as the car slid off again, with the man still on board.

'Freddie Exton,' whispered Rebecca. He was a famous business tycoon. Margaret Exton was being brought back to school in luxury, with the services of a chauffeur at her disposal. 'Lucky old Margaret!' she added.

The Fifth Year girl walked across the gravel and then pushed her way through the middle of them saying: 'What are you all gawping at, then?'

Rebecca thought she looked rather pale and later

she found out that Margaret Exton wasn't so lucky after all.

While Rebecca unpacked upstairs, Mara showed them some of the lovely new dresses she had brought back with her from Athens. 'Oh, Mara, I don't know when you'll get to wear them all!' laughed Tish.

'The white one's beautiful!' gasped Rebecca. 'Is that for the Commem Ball?'

Mara nodded happily.

'And what will you wear, Rebecca? Will you wear

something new, something Robbie has never seen you in before?'

'No such luck,' mumbled Rebecca. But she was looking forward to the Ball, every bit as much as Mara. It was one of the high spots of the summer term at Trebizon.

'I don't think I'll be going,' said Tish suddenly. 'I hope I'll have better things to do, that day,' she added, mysteriously.

'Oh –?' began Rebecca.

At that moment Elf appeared through the connecting door that led from the adjoining room, Margot just behind her. She was waving a small round cake tin above her head and smiling plumply.

'Found it!' she cried.

'It was in a bag with her games stuff,' added Margot.

'Yum, yum, *yum*,' said Rebecca, as Elf opened the tin and handed it round. 'I *love* home-made fudge.'

In a short while they'd all be getting tea, over in the school dining hall, but Rebecca didn't think she could last that long. She was starving. Long journeys always made her hungry.

'Mmmm. Delicious.'

The five of them sat around on the beds in the

big room, sucking the succulent fudge and talking non-stop about all the things that had happened in the holidays. It was some minutes before Rebecca noticed something.

'Oh. Then she's *back*? I thought she must be on the late train –' she said. She'd suddenly seen the suitcase, sticking out from under the bed. She added: 'Where's Sue, Tish?'

'Over at the Hilary,' replied Tish. 'Helping Holly Thomas with her violin.'

'Is she really?' exclaimed Rebecca.

She smiled and raised her eyebrows slightly. Tish smiled back.

For, of course, they both knew the reason why.

TWO
A Little Jolt

Sue Murdoch had met Justin Thomas at Tish's fifteenth birthday party. This had taken place towards the end of the holidays and of course Rebecca had been invited, too.

Tish had telephoned Rebecca at her grandmother's bungalow in Gloucestershire, from her own home in Hertfordshire.

'Rebeck, you have GOT to come – you'll have to stay the weekend.'

'How?' asked Rebecca anxiously. Her grandmother didn't drive.

'Robbie's worked it all out, it fits beautifully. He's going to be in Oxford on Saturday – one of the colleges is having an Open Day or something – and he says from where you live you can get a coach straight through to Oxford and there's one that arrives at Gloucester Green Bus Station at five –'

'Is there really?' said Rebecca, feeling a flutter of excitement. This was all news to her. 'And Robbie's got the car fixed again?'

'Worked at the farm over Easter, double pay, bought a reconditioned engine,' said Tish crisply. 'So he's going to pick you up from the Bus Station in Oxford on Saturday, okay? Go and ask your gran!'

Old Mrs Mason agreed readily and before ringing off, Rebecca said:

'Tell Robbie I'll see him in Oxford, then! So he's starting to visit colleges already? Oh, Tish, wasn't it good news for him? Being picked for the Oxbridge group? He was hoping and praying he would be.'

'My brother must be quite brainy, after all,' said Tish briefly.

But when Robbie collected Rebecca on the Saturday, in the heart of the bustling city, and she asked eagerly: 'Where are all the colleges, Robbie? Can we have a quick look? Where's the one you've been to today?' – he just shook his head.

He bundled her off to where he'd parked the car – and then they drove away. He was wearing jacket and tie, Rebecca noticed, and his unruly dark curly hair had been plastered down with some kind of gel. Negotiating the busy streets with their traffic lights and junctions, he was pale and uncommunicative and seemed to be deep in thought.

But once they were clear of the city, he visibly relaxed.

'Take a look behind you, Becky, Isn't it beautiful?'

Craning her head round, Rebecca caught a glimpse of shimmering spires and towers on the Oxford skyline, far behind them now.

'Oh, I wish there'd been time to see things!' said Rebecca in a disappointed voice. 'Have you chosen which college you want to try for yet?'

'Yes,' said Robbie.

'The one you've looked at today?'

'Yes.'

'Oh, Robbie, why wouldn't you let me have a peep at it?'

'Because I don't want to tempt fate,' he replied.

Rebecca contemplated that and after a while, she said:

'Is the competition going to be that bad, Robbie?'

'Horrendous,' he replied. 'There were hundreds there today. And they've got two more Open Days to come. Quite apart from the fact that a lot of people apply without even coming to an Open Day.'

'Well, at least you've got into the Oxbridge group at school,' said Rebecca, in a small voice. 'They think you're good enough to sit the entrance exam – and you'll be given tons of extra work for it, and special lessons.'

'So will all the others,' said Robbie. 'All over the country. Most of them, anyway.' He glanced at her and grinned. 'The entrance exam isn't till November, but I've seen some of the back papers. Phew–have I got to work!'

Although Robbie was in the Sixth Form at Garth College, a school very close to Trebizon, it dawned on Rebecca then that they probably wouldn't see much of each other during the coming term – not with her tennis and Robbie's Oxbridge work. Towards the end of the drive, Robbie referred to this obliquely.

'You know Justy Thomas has got into the Oxbridge group, too?' he said. 'Well, he's a bit depressed. So I've asked him over to Tish's party tonight. I thought it might cheer him up.'

'Depressed because he's got into the Oxbridge group?' asked Rebecca in surprise.

'No, not because of that,' Robbie said. 'Hasn't

Tish told you? Laura Wilkins has broken it off with him. Says he takes life much too seriously and is becoming a workaholic! Mike Brown wrote to her in the holidays and asked if he could take her to your Commem Ball this year, and that clinched it.'

'Mike did?' exclaimed Rebecca. Mike was in the Fourth Year at Garth and a lot of fun; he was one of a crowd they sometimes met up with. 'So he likes Laura? The dark horse!' She thought about it for a moment, then said: 'Oh dear, I hope Sue won't be put out. Mike's always been her reliable stand-by.'

Robbie appeared not to have heard that, because he said:

'So I'm booking you up for the Commem right *now*, Rebecca. Okay?'

'Consider me booked!' said Rebecca. And she laughed happily.

Later, at Tish's party, Rebecca decided that Robbie must have taken in her comment about Sue after all, because he made a special point of introducing Justin Thomas to her. They knew each other by sight only and were, in fact, sitting in adjacent armchairs and taking no notice of one another, each wrapped in their own thoughts and listening to some of the tapes. Justin was brooding heavily about Laura and

Sue was, indeed, slightly put out to have heard the news about Mike Brown – even though there had never been anything romantic between them. Apart from anything else it had meant Tish not inviting him to the party, even though he lived fairly near. 'I can't now that Robbie's asked Justin Thomas, Sue,' she'd explained. 'Justy's the emotional type – he might decide to clock him one.'

But after Robbie had introduced them, Sue and Justin both seemed to cheer up and were talking together for quite a long time.

'He's really nice, isn't he?' Sue said casually to Tish and Rebecca later, as the three of them washed up some of the cups and glasses. 'We both like the same composers!'

'What were you talking about all that time?' asked Tish, curious.

Sue pushed her spectacles up her nose; they had slipped a little.

'We talked a bit about Holly,' she said. 'He doesn't think she's settled in at Trebizon all that well. You know she's got a slight limp – she was run over by a car when she was nine – well, Sarah Butters and one or two others tease her about it.'

'I've heard them,' said Tish. 'The little horrors call her Holly Hobble. I've told them to shut up.'

'Well, the doctors say she should do gym and running and everything quite normally, and that would actually improve the leg, but in fact she does as little as possible because she's scared of being laughed at.'

'Oh, what a shame,' said Rebecca. 'Poor Holly.' She mused about it. The little First Year girl was small for her age and very unprepossessing to look at. Her brother was handsome, in a sensitive, poetic kind of way – and her big sister, Della, last year's

Senior Prefect at Trebizon, had been stunning to look at, as well as good as everything! 'And she's got Justin and Della to live up to.'

'That makes it worse, I'm sure,' agreed Sue.

'Well, I'm a bit surprised at Sarah Butters,' said Tish, quite unsentimentally. 'But Holly's got to learn to stand up for herself – just laugh right back in their faces. You get that sort of thing in the First Year.'

'Well, I've said I'll keep an eye on Holly for him, anyway!' Sue confessed. 'He's going to ring me up sometimes and I'll keep him posted.'

'What, Justy asked you to take Holly under your wing?' inquired Tish, with interest.

'Well, no, I – I sort of offered,' mumbled Sue, looking embarrassed.

Behind Sue's back, Rebecca and Tish had exchanged secret smiles.

And now, back at school for the new term, they were once again smiling at each other.

So Sue was already over at the Hilary, helping Holly with violin practice? It seemed that she hadn't wasted a moment. She intended keeping her promise to Justin Thomas.

While Sue was doing that and Rebecca and Co. were lounging around in the big room at Court House, eating fudge, Miss Welbeck was receiving Margaret Exton's father in her study, over in the main building.

'I'm so grateful that you could spare the time to come and see me, Mr Exton,' said the Principal of Trebizon School, 'so that we can talk over Margaret's future together and I can explain the situation fully. Do please sit down –' She nodded towards the chair. 'Won't you sit down?'

Instead of sitting down, the burly business tycoon came right up to Miss Welbeck's desk, and produced his cheque book, resting it on the corner of the desk while he unscrewed the cap of his very expensive gold-tipped fountain pen.

'Now, Miss Welbeck,' he said with a genial smile, although the smile was not reflected in the small, cold eyes, 'before we get down to our chat, I'd be very grateful if you'd accept a donation to the school's Magazine Fund. I'm sure it must need topping up by now and I intend to do it proud, just as I did once before –'

'Please, Mr Exton.' Miss Welbeck's hand shot across the desk and rested, palm down, on the open cheque book, before her visitor could start to write. He stared at her in surprise, and she met his gaze, unflinchingly. 'Your generosity to the school over the years has been greatly appreciated,' she said quietly. 'But I have to make it clear to you, Mr Exton, that in no circumstances whatsoever am I able to take Margaret into the Sixth Form in September.'

'You took Elizabeth in!' he said, suddenly becoming aggressive.

'Of course. She was suited to Sixth Form work. It was tragic that she behaved as badly as she did and had to leave before taking her A levels. But in Margaret's case –'

'Margaret's kept on the rails!' said the man. 'You're punishing her because of her sister's record –'

'What preposterous nonsense!' exclaimed the Principal. Then, gently: 'Can't you understand, Mr Exton, that it would be extremely unkind of both of us to allow Margaret to spend two years in the Sixth Form, and a total waste of time for everyone concerned, most of all for Margaret herself. From the results of mock GCSEs in January it's absolutely crystal clear that she will not be able to cope with Sixth Form work and would simply spend two very miserable years here. What I want to discuss with you this afternoon are the many possibilities that exist for her elsewhere. I have a list of training courses that I know would be suitable for her –'

Freddie Exton picked up his cheque book, slowly closed it and put it away, along with his pen. He was staring at Miss Welbeck in uncomprehending anger, hardly listening to a word that she was saying.

'You're throwing her out then?' he said, jaw sagging in surprise. 'She's got to leave this summer, after her GCSEs? What's the point of my paying fees all these years to send my daughter to a good school if –' his voice began to rise in anger '– if she's not allowed to go right through. How's *this* going to look on her record! Didn't you do Elizabeth enough damage –'

'Please calm down,' said the Principal icily. 'I think at least for Margaret's sake we should discuss her future options quietly and sensibly . . .'

'I don't want to discuss anything,' he said. 'Good afternoon to you.'

He turned on his heel and marched out of the oak-panelled study, slamming the door behind him. His face was a pale purple colour.

Miss Welbeck leant back in her chair, gripping the wooden arms, trembling very slightly. It had been a most unpleasant interview. Quite an ordeal. One did one's best.

But hard decisions had to be taken sometimes. Parents often found them difficult to accept. This wasn't the first time.

And it probably wouldn't be the last.

It was Sue who was the first to hear the news. She'd walked across to the dining hall from Court House with Moyra Milton, who was a Fifth Year in Court. In fact Moyra's study cubicle was right next door to Margaret Exton's, on the top floor. Sue and Moyra got on well: they were both Music Scholars at Trebizon and played in the school orchestra together.

Rebecca and Co. had looked into the Hilary Camberwell Music School on their way to tea, hoping to pick Sue up there – but they'd just missed her. She'd gone back to Court by a different route to dump her violin and so had walked to the dining hall with Moyra instead.

'Guess what!' said Sue, in a hushed voice, slipping into the seat they'd saved for her at one of the tables. 'Freddie Exton got a summons from Miss Welbeck today. She wanted to talk over Margaret's future prospects! They had a terrible row! Guess what her future prospects are –'

'What?' asked Elf, leaning forward, wide-eyed.

'She's being chucked out at the end of this term!' whispered Sue. 'Apparently she failed all her mocks in January.' Sue turned and looked along the table to where Rebecca was sitting. '*Hi*, Rebecca! Pass me some of that cheese and bacon pie, I'm starving.'

Rebecca did so, but her hand was shaking very slightly. 'Good riddance!' Tish was saying, but Rebecca wasn't listening.

We've been summonsed. That's what her father's letter had said. *Miss Welbeck wants to see us ... have a talk about your future prospects, Becky.* She'd been rather pleased about that, but suddenly she wasn't so sure. She'd taken it for granted that it was good news but supposing – just supposing – it wasn't? Why *had* she taken it for granted? She was only just holding her own in maths and as for the science subjects, she was slipping badly in those. Definitely.

It gave Rebecca a nasty little jolt.

But then, from the next table, Josselyn Vining called across – and Rebecca's slight unease vanished almost as quickly as it had come.

THREE
Tish Makes a Suggestion

'Congratulations, Rebecca!' called Joss, above the hubbub in the school dining hall. It was always noisier than usual at the first sitting after the holidays – four hundred girls catching up on each other's news!

Joss radiated good health and physical fitness and her serious, pretty face was lit by a smile as she waved to Rebecca. Rebecca, turning round to see who had called to her, waved across in delight.

'Welcome back, Joss!'

Turning back to her tea, Rebecca said to Tish:

'Joss is back for good, now. Hurray! I've got someone brilliant to play against, again. I know she's better than me, but I think I'm going to be much better competition for her now. I bet we'll have some really good games.'

'It's going to be interesting,' said Tish.

She knew that Rebecca was longing to pit herself against Josselyn Vining who, even before a year's special tennis coaching in the United States, had been one of the top players in her age group in the whole of Britain. At that time Rebecca, although already showing early signs of exceptional talent, could barely take a game off her. But in the thirteen months that had elapsed since then Rebecca, ten months younger than Joss, had caught up in height and strength and was considered by everyone who understood the game to have made very exciting progress. So how would she match up to Joss now?

'Is it true she might be going in an England youth team next season?' asked Elf, who was sitting on the other side of the table, opposite Tish. They were talking about hockey now. 'I saw Laura Wilkins just now and she said something about some selectors being at the seven-a-sides tournament you went to at the end of last term.'

'Yes, I heard that too,' said Tish. 'At least, I heard that they're going to want her for trials some time, now she's home again.'

'That girl is a *paragon*!' exclaimed Mara. 'She is

pretty and clever as well. And nice. And brilliant at the long jump! It is not *fair*.'

'Cheer up, Mara,' said Rebecca, laughing. 'She's not as pretty as you.'

'Nor as rich!' added Margot. The black girl gave a wicked smile.

They all laughed. Rebecca was feeling happy again. It was good to have Joss back at Trebizon. A paragon. In Italian, Mr Pargiter had once told her, the word *paragone* actually meant touchstone ... wasn't that odd? Mr Pargiter was supposed to teach them Latin, not Italian, but he often digressed and talked about words in general, which was one of the reasons why Rebecca liked his lessons so much. It was in Rebecca's nature to store up off-beat pieces of information and she reflected that Joss, to her, as well as being a paragon was a *paragone* – a touchstone.

In fact they had to go to a tennis meeting together, straight after tea. Miss Willis, the head of the games staff, announced it in hall.

'Trisha Martyn would like to see the following girls over in the sports centre *now* please ...' She read five names from a piece of a paper, Rebecca's and Joss's amongst them.

They ran over there together to see what it was all about.

Trisha Martyn was in the Upper Sixth and the school's Head of Games this year. Looking glamorous in a white tracksuit she greeted Rebecca and Joss with a smile. The other three, Lady Edwina Burton, Alison Hissup and Suky Morris, were there ahead of them.

'Right, just a quick meeting,' she said. 'Caxton High phoned Miss Darling this afternoon and suggested a friendly this Saturday, if we can get a team together. So the tennis season's off to a quick start! Is everybody here free on Saturday?' She looked at Rebecca and Joss. 'No county tennis?'

'Not till Sunday,' Rebecca said, quickly and eagerly.

'There's Athletics Club,' Joss pointed out, rather to everyone's surprise.

'Then you'll just have to miss it, won't you,' said Trisha. 'I want you and Rebecca to play as first pair.'

Rebecca drew in a quick breath.

This was just what Elf had predicted! But Rebecca herself had been far from sure . . .

'What about you then, Trisha?' she asked shyly.

'I think you're probably better than me by now, Rebecca,' replied the Head of Games. 'Besides, I haven't a hope of getting to Eastbourne in my age group, while you have in yours. So we want to give you the hardest matches we can this term. It's all going to help.'

Rebecca regarded her in silent gratitude.

'And so,' continued Trisha, 'I think Eddie and I should play second pair – Alison and Suky can play third. It's all a bit flung together at this stage, but it's only a friendly. We'll see how things go.'

'Can you and Eddie give us a game tomorrow, then?' asked Joss. 'Rebecca and I have never partnered each other before.'

It was all arranged.

Rebecca walked back across the school grounds with Joss. The other girl was in Norris House, which lay at the back of Court. It was cool now, for an evening breeze had sprung up, sighing through the branches of the avenue of sycamore trees where they walked.

'I'm looking forward to playing you this term,' Rebecca confessed at last, breaking the silence. 'I hope I can give you a good game now – better than I used to.'

'Not urgent, though,' responded Joss. 'If we're partners, let's get to play *with* each other – never

mind *against* each other. *I'm* quite looking forward to *that*.'

'So am I!' said Rebecca and smiled. 'Do you think we can beat them, Trisha and Eddie?'

'We'll look pretty rubbish if we can't,' replied Joss.

'Of course,' nodded Rebecca.

But as they split up and she watched Joss stroll across to the side gate that led into Norris, a far away expression in her eyes, Rebecca had the distinct impression that her mind was on other things, not even on tennis at all.

It obviously hadn't impinged on her just *how much* Rebecca wanted to play against her. Well, Rebecca wasn't going to press it. The whole of the summer term stretched ahead of them.

She could afford to be patient.

'In the meantime: I'm going to find the others and tell them the news!' she thought happily. 'Oh, isn't life wonderful!'

Tish thought life was wonderful, too.

She was lying on her bed in her tracksuit, on her back, legs stretched up in the air and looking very relaxed.

'I've just been to Mulberry Cove and back and I'm not even out of breath,' she said. 'Would you say that's 1500 metres? I'm looking forward to Athletics Club on Saturday. I'm going to ask Angela Hessel if I can try the 1500 metres this term.'

'What, instead of the 800?' asked Rebecca with interest.

'No, as well as,' said Tish.

'What a marvellous idea –' began Rebecca. And then, as Mara came into the room with her white dress for the Commem Ball (she had just been along to the single room to show it to Fiona Freeman), it brought something back to mind for Rebecca. 'Tish, what did you mean earlier about not going to Commem this year and hoping you'd have something better to do?'

Tish laughed, clapped her hands and then sat up straight.

'Rebecca, you're a mind reader, you really are!' she said, looking across at her.

'Why, has it got something to do with running 1500 metres?'

'Yes!'

Tish explained that she'd seen the term's Athletics calendar over at the sports centre, earlier that day, and there was to be a West of England athletics meeting on the same day as Commemoration, always the last Saturday in June. The high point of the meeting was to be a 1500 metres race – minimum age fifteen years.

'I'd have to qualify, of course,' said Tish wryly, 'so I think that means a lot of hard work. But I'd love to have a go! If by any chance I got accepted for the race – well, the meeting's in the evening, so I wouldn't be able to go to the Commem Ball as well, would I? Even supposing there were anyone I wanted to go with,' she added as an afterthought.

She glanced across at Sue who was engrossed in the task of applying rosin to the bow of her violin.

'What about Edward?' said Sue, referring to the elder of her two brothers. He and Tish got on quite well. 'If you're desperate, I mean,' she added hastily.

Tish laughed and there was a light in her eye. 'I'm going to see how I get on with the 1500 metres first!'

Mara and Rebecca exchanged indulgent looks. Tish had a new craze now: she was going to try a new distance. She would be quite single-minded about it; nothing would deflect her. Tish was like that.

'Well, Rebecca and I are going,' declared Mara. 'And so is Sue, I expect.' She glanced across the room. 'Will you go with Mike Brown?'

'He's taking Laura Wilkins,' said Sue, without even bothering to look up. She drew the bow across her violin, testing it. As Mara exclaimed with interest, Sue quickly closed the subject by saying: 'Quite a surprise, eh? Who'd have thought old Mike could be so romantic – he wrote to her in the holidays.'

'Then you're not upset –?' began Mara.

'Not in the least!' said Sue. She gave a brief smile. 'Apart from anything else, he's a terrible dancer. He treads on your toes! No, seriously, if I could choose anybody I wanted to take me to Commem, then I think Mike's the last person I'd choose. I really *don't* mind.'

She meant it. The Fourth Year boy at Garth College no longer occupied a place in Sue's thoughts – to Rebecca, that was obvious.

'Well, who *would* you choose then?' asked Mara.

'Oh, I don't know.' Sue appeared to be concentrating hard on slackening the bow, before putting it away. She shrugged. 'Nobody in particular,' she said quickly. 'Don't suppose I'll even go.'

* * *

Sue did *not* think life was wonderful.

Rebecca discovered that just before bedtime when, crashing into the bathroom with her washbag, she almost collided with Sue, who was standing in front of the bathroom mirror in her dressing gown, her face full of woe.

'I'm so plain,' she pronounced. 'Mind-bendingly plain - and pasty faced. *And* I wear glasses. *And* I'm getting out of condition.'

'Sue!'

Rebecca burst out laughing in surprise.

'What a lot of rubbish!' she exclaimed. 'None of that's true and you know it, except the bit about wearing glasses and they suit you anyway. You've got the best figure of all of us, you look like a model even when you're wearing school uniform, you've got the most lovely sandy-coloured hair and – oh, Sue. You've got high cheekbones!' Rebecca caught a glimpse of her own face in the mirror and felt woeful herself, just for a moment. 'Oh, I wish I had high cheekbones. My face is sort of round and ordinary-looking, compared to yours . . .'

Sue turned round to face Rebecca, already looking more cheerful.

'You honestly don't think I'm plain?' she inquired.

'Of *course* not, Sue.'

'But I *am* out of condition and not getting enough exercise,' said Sue, stubbornly. She raised one leg and then, bending it at the knee, she looked back over her shoulder and pinched her calf. 'Look at this flab. It used to be muscle! What should I do about it? Do you think I should go jogging –?'

'Of course you should!' exclaimed Tish, suddenly appearing in the bathroom door, washbag at the ready. She was grinning. 'Every morning, before breakfast. So should you, Rebeck. You've got to be super-fit if you're going to get to Eastbourne, haven't you?'

'Oh, let's do that!' said Rebecca eagerly. 'Evenings as well. Every evening before tea. Come on, Sue. It'll do you good.'

'Shall we?' said Sue. She looked enthusiastic, completely cheerful again. 'It'll do my complexion good as well, won't it? Lots of fresh air. Maybe the six of us but *at least* us three! We've all got a good reason, haven't we?'

'Especially me,' said Tish. Then, giving Sue a thoughtful glance, she said: 'Perhaps we could take little Holly Thomas with us sometimes. Just for a bit of the way. She might come, early in the morning, when there's nobody around to see her.'

'Oh, Tish – what a *lovely* idea!' exclaimed Sue.

'Will she be able to keep up with us?' asked Rebecca anxiously.

'She can just do five minutes with us,' suggested Sue. 'We can slow down for her. As she gets better we'll let her stay longer.'

'Great,' agreed Rebecca.

It seemed such a good idea at the time.

FOUR
Perigee Tides

However on the very first run, the next morning, it was just the three of them on their own. Mara didn't want to come. 'You are mad!' she stated, pulling the duvet over her head when she heard them moving around the room before seven o'clock, climbing into their tracksuits and hunting for training shoes. 'I am perfectly fit, thank you very much.'

When they looked into the adjoining room, Elf was snoring peacefully and Margot, opening one eye, said: 'Are you joking?'

As for the possibility of Holly coming on these runs, that had yet to be arranged.

So, each for their own reason, Rebecca, Tish and Sue jogged elbow to elbow through the school grounds and then down into the bay, scrambling over the dunes and catapulting themselves on to the wide sands. It was the loveliest spring morning, the sea calm and without any early mist, the whole of Trebizon Bay golden and empty and newly washed by the receding tide and the air exceptionally clear and shimmering after some rain in the night. 'Oh, isn't this wonderful!' exclaimed Rebecca as the three of them pounded along the shore in single file.

It was so exhilarating, that first run of term, it made Rebecca secretly regret Tish's idea about Holly Thomas. It wouldn't be quite the same, having to hang around for a First Year, even for just part of the time. She knew she was being churlish.

And just one look at Holly's face, when the three of them found her during the dinner break that day, banished Rebecca's lingering doubts. To be able to bring such happiness!

'Do you mean it?' said the First Year girl, her face animated with excitement and pleasure.

They had found her curled up reading a book in the First Year Common Room, upstairs in Juniper House, where all the juniors lived. She was sitting alone by the window, which had a pleasant outlook on to the quadrangle gardens at the back which stretched across to main school. Even viewed from the back the former manor house was delightful on the eye, Rebecca thought, and she could imagine maids and butlers and footmen, scurrying in and out of those servants' quarters in earlier days, leading their separate existence from the grand life that went on in the front of the house.

Holly, quite alone in the Common Room, was a thin scrap of a girl, small for her age, with wispy fair hair that tended to straggle in her eyes. She had looked up nervously as they'd entered – but now her pale face with its rather withdrawn expression was quite transformed, pretty even. 'Do you really *mean* it?' she repeated.

'Of course we mean it!' said Sue. 'It'd do you good. Justin's worried about you always getting out of games. You're silly.'

'Will we be seen?' asked Holly anxiously, then.

'No, of course we won't,' said Tish. 'Not so early in the morning. Come on then, Holly.' She took the girl by the hand and pulled her to her feet in the usual purposeful Tish manner. 'Let's go and find Matron or someone and get permission for tomorrow morning. Then it'll be all settled.'

Alice, a young assistant matron, was vacuuming one of the dormitories and readily gave her permission. 'Early morning run on the beach tomorrow? Why not? Yes, that's perfectly okay, Holly.'

They agreed to meet Holly at a quarter past seven the next morning, by the little wicket gate at the back of Juniper House that led out into Trebizon Bay; so it *was* all settled.

'You hardly notice her limp,' commented Rebecca, as the three of them walked over to main school for afternoon lessons. 'Isn't it a shame she's so self-conscious about it.'

'I'm sure it'll do her confidence good,' said Sue. 'She'll soon find she can run as well as any of them. Justin says she can. It's all a matter of getting her started.'

'You two coming out again before tea?' asked Tish, changing the subject.

'I've got a tennis match!' said Rebecca, putting her hand to her mouth. 'Oh, that's not a good start, is it?'

'And I'm down for a violin lesson!' smiled Sue.

'Oh, never mind. I'll just go on my own then,' said Tish, happily. Then: 'Come on, Rebeck, stop dawdling or we'll be late for Latin.'

'And I'll be late for music!' exclaimed Sue.

Joss and Rebecca beat Trisha and Eddie, but not as conclusively as they should have done. In fact they'd had to struggle at times.

'They're used to playing together and we're not,' Joss pointed out afterwards. 'Didn't we make a mess of the first set? Both rushing to the centre at the same time and leaving great gaps at the sides of the court.'

'I'm just glad we've had a practice together before we play Caxton on Saturday,' said Rebecca.

All in all it had been exciting partnering a player of Joss's calibre, though surprisingly she had missed some easy volleys. As they split up in the dining hall to go to their respective tables, Rebecca realised that she still felt as fresh as a daisy. She must be fit. How undemanding doubles were, compared with singles.

'I'm starving!' she said, as she sat down. 'Don't eat all the jacket potatoes, Elf; pass some over.' She looked round the table. 'Where's Tish?'

'She's late,' said Mara. 'We thought she must have gone on to watch your game. Did you win, Rebecca?'

'Must be still out running,' mumbled Sue through some lettuce.

In fact Tish was almost fifteen minutes late for tea. She sidled in through the glass doors and tried to dart across to the table without being seen, but a voice from a Fifth Year table called out: 'You're supposed to sign the late book, Tish Anderson.'

Margaret Exton.

'Trust her!' whispered Mara furiously.

Sheepishly Tish went back and signed the late book and then came and joined them at table; she was slightly out of breath from running and Rebecca noticed that her trainers had left wet footprints on the wood block flooring.

'Where have you been?' she said.

Tish shrugged. 'Just late, that's all.' But there was a very slightly guilty expression on her face and Rebecca noted it.

She noted exactly the same expression shortly before bedtime when, picking up a note pad that had fallen off Tish's locker, she couldn't help noticing something written in block capitals:

N.B. FIND OUT ABOUT PERIGEE TIDES.

'Here, give me that, Becky!' said Tish. 'It's mine.'

'I'm just giving it to you!' said Rebecca indignantly.

But she was mildly intrigued. What had perigee tides got to do with anything – and what was so secret about them, anyway?

'Whatever it is, I expect Tish will tell us sooner or

later,' she thought with a smile, as she settled down to read in bed for ten minutes before going to sleep. It was an Agatha Christie, borrowed from Margot, and Rebecca reckoned that she had already worked out who the murderer must be (but was eager to see if she were correct) so dismissed all further conjecture about Tish from her mind.

'Don't read all night, Rebecca,' Sue called across, 'remember we've got to be up early in the morning.'

'Crazy people!' laughed Mara.

Sue flung her pillow across at her. 'Lazy lump!' she shouted. 'It's all right for you, you look good all the time in spite of the fact that you never take any exercise at all, as far as I can see.'

Mara laughed again, brown eyes shining as she threw Sue's pillow back to her.

'That is not true, Susan Murdoch,' she shouted back. 'I like dancing.'

'Shut up, you two,' wailed Rebecca. 'I'm trying to read.'

But she was secretly pleased to notice that Sue was in such high spirits. It must be because they were seeing Holly in the morning and because of Sue's promise to Justin Thomas.

They collected the First Year girl, self-conscious in an over-large and very new looking Trebizon track-suit, at the little gate at the bottom of the copse at the back of Juniper House, early next morning as arranged. And their first work-out together could not have been more of a success.

'You could be a good runner!' said Tish, impressed. They had only jogged as far as the beach huts and back, but Holly had kept up with them quite well, even though she was now rather out of breath. 'That leg of yours looked fine to me!'

'Was I really all right?' puffed Holly. There was a breeze whipping off the sea this morning and her cheeks had a healthy glow to them now. 'I couldn't run a step further, though.'

'Better get back now, Holly, if you don't want anyone to see you,' said Sue, kindly. 'Though goodness knows why not!'

'I want to get reasonable first!' said Holly. 'Then I won't mind if they know I've taken up running.'

'Good for you,' nodded Rebecca. 'See you tomorrow then?'

'Same time, same place!' said Sue.

'Bye!'

And, their duty discharged, the three friends

raced off together in the direction of Mulberry Cove
for a long and exhilarating run.

This continued for some days, plenty of running
morning and evening, but including Holly for part
of the time in the early morning, watching her
gradually improve, with determination written all
over her face.

The weekend came and went and Rebecca was
particularly pleased with herself. The running seemed
to be keeping her very fit. She and Joss beat Caxton
High's first pair on the Saturday with relative ease,
even though their opponents were both eighteen,

and on the Sunday when they went to Exonford for junior county tennis, they each won their respective singles against a neighbouring county.

Joss was expected to, of course. She had been given back her old Number One county ranking after her year's absence and made short work of her opposite number. Rebecca, now ranked Number Two, was pleased and surprised to win her match as easily as she did.

When she got back to Court House on the Sunday evening, she found a radiant Sue. Justin Thomas had telephoned her during the afternoon and they had talked for nearly twenty minutes downstairs, until there had been a queue of people waiting to use the payphone.

'He's *really* pleased that we're taking Holly out running,' said Sue. 'Oh, and guess what, he says he'll try and drop over here next weekend if he can, and will I give him coffee?'

'Isn't everything going well, Sue,' said Rebecca happily. Because, to cap it all, Angela Hessel had timed Tish over 1500 metres at Athletics Club on Saturday and told her she was a natural at the distance.

By the following Tuesday, Holly insisted on

running all the way across the bay and back and, although her limp was rather pronounced by the end, it was just the breakthrough that they'd been hoping for. Self-confidence was definitely starting to emerge.

'I've decided I don't mind if anyone sees me now,' she pronounced. 'I'm getting much better, aren't I? And guess what – you know it's Junior Charity Week in a fortnight's time? Well, some of them are organising a sponsored run and I'm going to put my name down for it tomorrow!'

'Oh, Holly, that's wonderful!' said Sue.

'I'll sponsor you!' said Rebecca.

'Can I come running with you this afternoon, then?' asked Holly. She knew the three of them jogged before tea most evenings, for she had watched them wistfully at times, longing to join in but not daring to until now. 'Would you mind? Just for ten minutes? I don't care if they see me!' she repeated.

The three friends exchanged glances and then nodded.

'Sure.'

So they took Holly on a run round the school grounds on the Tuesday evening – and when they passed a little knot of girls that included Sarah

Butters, there was no jeering, just an impressed silence. Holly was going along well, no doubt about it. She was limping a little bit, but not so's you'd notice.

'Hi, Holly!' called Sarah Butters, finding her voice at last. 'Why don't you go in for the sponsored run?'

'I'm thinking about it!' Holly called back over her shoulder. 'You going to sponsor me?'

'If you like!'

Rebecca and Co. were delighted. They were even more pleased when, on the Wednesday morning, before they parted, Holly said: 'Don't worry about me coming this afternoon. Harriet Baker's put her name down for the sponsored run as well and she's asked me if I'd like to go and practise with her on the track. Seeing it's going to be on the school track, it's best for me to get some practice there now, isn't it?'

'Of course it is!' said Sue.

'You still going to sponsor me, Rebecca?' asked the First Year girl shyly.

'How about ten pence a lap?' asked Rebecca.

Holly nodded eagerly.

'I'll sponsor Harriet Baker, if you like,' said Tish.

'Tell her to bring her form over to Court House tomorrow.'

'Great, thanks!'

Holly was already hurrying away, scrambling over the sand dunes in the direction of Juniper House, presumably to tell her new-found friend that she'd found a sponsor for her.

'Why don't you *both* bring your forms to Court tomorrow?' called Sue. 'We'll go round and twist a few arms for you.'

'Can we really? Oh, thanks, Sue!'

And she scrambled away all the faster.

That evening, when the three of them were out jogging again before tea, Tish said to Sue:

'I don't suppose Holly will manage more than two or three laps, but the main thing is she's going to have a go.'

'And she seems to have made friends with Harriet Baker!' put in Rebecca. 'Even if some of them do laugh at her, I don't think she'll mind now – and when they see she doesn't mind, it won't be any fun laughing at her any more.'

'This is going to be such a relief to Justin,' said Sue.

They had come to a halt on top of the headland

that overlooked Mulberry Cove. 'What are you staring at, Sue?' asked Rebecca and followed her gaze. In fact Sue had just been staring into space, seeing nothing, just thinking about Justin. But Rebecca, looking in the same direction, actually *did* see something.

'Hey – look at that!' she said.

'We'd better get back now,' said Tish hastily. 'Nearly tea time.'

'Oh, not yet, Tish,' said Rebecca, grabbing her arm. 'Look over there – look at the island. It's hardly an island at all!'

She gazed, fascinated, at Mulberry Island which lay about half a mile out from the cove. The sea which usually cut it off from the mainland had today all but disappeared. The sand ran out all the way to the island, save for a narrow strip of sea no wider than a river which breached the land halfway between the mainland and the island. 'I've never seen it like that before!' cried Rebecca.

'We could almost *walk* there,' said Sue.

Tish turned away: 'Just exceptional spring tides, that's all,' she mumbled. 'Come on. Let's get back.'

She looked rather shifty; Rebecca had seen that faintly guilty expression before – and two words clicked in her memory. 'Perigee tides!' she said out loud. 'That's it, isn't it, Tish?'

She and Sue both hauled Tish back, intrigued.

'What *are* you being secretive about?' laughed Rebecca. 'Sorry, Tish. I couldn't help seeing that note you'd written last week!'

Tish blurted it out then. She was so excited, she couldn't stop herself.

'There's going to be perigee tides tomorrow, one in the morning and one in the evening. The one at five-thirty is going to be the lowest for years. All the land's going to be completely uncovered for twenty minutes!' she said. 'If you must know, I'm going to run to the island and back – oh grief, I've told you now and I didn't want to. I'll get a rocket if anybody finds out, but I've got to do it. I know I can run fast enough. It'll be easy!'

'Tish!' said Sue, pretending to sound shocked. She and Rebecca exchanged amused glances.

'Are you daring to suggest,' said Rebecca, in just the same tone as Sue, 'are you daring to suggest –'

'Oh, don't be spoilsports!' wailed Tish. 'Don't try and stop me.'

'Are you daring to suggest that we *can't* run fast enough?' finished Rebecca.

She and Sue burst out laughing.

'If you think you're going to leave us out of an adventure like this,' said Sue, 'then you've got another think coming.'

It was going to be an adventure, all right.

FIVE
An Alarming Sight

It was most unfortunate, bumping into Holly and Miss Morgan like that, right at the last minute. It couldn't have been *more* unfortunate. But the three friends were so keyed up with excitement by then, so determined to run to Mulberry Island and back, in secret, that they weren't going to allow even *that* to stop them. They would never, never get the chance again!

All day Thursday, they hugged the secret to themselves. They thought about telling the other three, but decided against it. 'The more people who know, the more chance there is of getting found out,' said Tish. 'That's somebody-or-other's law. It's bad enough that there's *three* of us now –' She gave a bouncy smile. 'Instead of just me!'

'It's going to be marvellous fun!' said Rebecca. She felt a tremor of excitement every time she thought about it. She'd sailed close to Mulberry Island in a sailing boat the previous summer and had long been intrigued by the little ruined house there, once the home of an artist. Now the chance to explore it had come in the most unexpected way – though they'd have to be quick, of course.

When Holly and Harriet came over to Court with their sponsorship forms, during the dinner hour, they were relieved to hear Holly say: 'Me and Harriet are going down to the track again after school. On the day of the run, we want to surprise everyone with the number of laps we can do – don't we, Harri?'

Her new-found friend, a pleasant, plump-faced girl, not noted for her athletic prowess, nodded eagerly. Elf, Mara and Margot sponsored them – Mara particularly generously; ever since Justin's long phone call on Sunday, the other members of 'the six' had realised that this was rather a special business for Sue, taking Holly Thomas under her wing. Jenny Brook-Hayes, Aba Amori, Elizabeth Kendall and Fiona Freeman all chipped in as well – in fact, everyone who was around at the time.

That evening, as Rebecca and Co. strolled

towards Juniper House in tracksuits, intending to go on to the beach via the wicket gate there, Tish said: 'Lucky Holly didn't want to come running with *us* again, wasn't it?'

They were going at a leisurely pace, saving their energy for the race across to the island. The waters would be rolling back from the sea bed in exactly fifteen minutes' time. 'She'll be down at the track with Harriet now,' began Rebecca. 'Oh –'

As they rounded the corner of the big red brick building where all the juniors lived, they almost cannoned into Holly Thomas!

'Hello!' said Holly eagerly.

She'd been standing at the back of Juniper House talking to Miss Morgan, the House Mistress in charge of the Junior School. Holly was wearing her tracksuit, but there was no sign of Harriet.

'Oh, Sue, Sue! Can I come with you?' begged Holly. 'I got all changed for running, but some seniors are using the track! Harri's stayed to watch them, but I'm dying to do some running.'

'We're jogging all the way down to the town today!' said Tish quickly and with great presence of mind. 'It's much too far for you and besides, it's out of bounds for First and Second Years!'

'Sorry, Hol,' said Sue.

'Which way are you going to the town?' asked Miss Morgan.

'Oh, we hadn't decided –' began Tish. The three friends exchanged looks. What a horrible web of deceit they were getting enmeshed in. They didn't want to take the risk of Holly coming down on to the beach. 'We were wondering about the beach way,' said Tish, 'but on second thoughts we've decided to go along the top road. Haven't we?'

'Yes!' said Sue quickly.

'Much better that way,' added Rebecca. The top road was definitely out of bounds for the juniors, whereas part of the way, by the beach, was not. 'Come on, we'd better get going.'

Then to their consternation, Miss Morgan propelled Holly forward. She wanted to do everything possible to encourage the girl's new found interest in running – and it was good the way these three had helped her. But she could see how disappointed Holly was now.

'Well, why not let Holly tag along with you as far as the main gates?' she said. It wasn't so much a question, as a command. 'That won't be too far for her.'

'Oh – er, right,' said Tish. 'Right. Let's go.'

'Don't take her any further than the main gates, mind!'

'No, Miss Morgan!'

They turned away from Juniper House and set off by the quickest possible route across the grounds to the main gates that led out on to the coast road, with Holly Thomas in tow. It was going to take them a good five minutes.

'Oh, Tish, are we going to make it all right?' whispered Rebecca.

'I think so. As soon as we've ditched Holly at the gates, we can cut across the road there – there's a little path that drops down behind the headland and into Mulberry Cove. We should just about make it.'

When they reached the gates Holly said, 'I'm still fresh! I'm not a bit out of breath. Let me see how far I can run with you, *please* Sue. Let me show you!'

'No!' said Sue, quite snappily. 'Of course not. Shoo!'

They were so anxious about time by now that they didn't even wait to see if Holly turned back straight away. They just took it for granted that she would. They came out on to the top road, paused to make sure that it was free of traffic, then shot straight across without even looking back.

And that was another unfortunate thing.

Because Holly loitered by the high wrought-iron gates of Trebizon School, peering along the road, watching them as they ran. In her imagination she was running with them, keeping up with them, all the way down into the town . . .

Then her eyes grew round. Less than fifty metres along the road, they peeled off into some gorse bushes, shouting and laughing. There seemed to be some kind of little path there, that dropped down towards the sand dunes and, far beyond that, the sea. They weren't going to the town at all! They were going down to the sea.

She could have gone with them after all! She had loads and loads of energy left, she was hardly limping at all. Her leg was getting much stronger. Didn't they realise? Perhaps she should show them just *how* strong! Perhaps she could give them a surprise?

The reason that Rebecca and Co. were shouting and laughing was sheer relief, because one look at the distant, grey-crested sea told them that the tide was still going out.

And as they dropped down behind the headland and then into the secret empty silence of Mulberry Cove, sheltered from the wind, they were just in time to see the last finger of sea creep back from the sands beyond the cove – and Mulberry Island was an island no longer!

'Hurray!' said Tish.

This was perfect timing. They started to run, as fast as their legs would carry them. The tension of the past few minutes gave the adventure even more excitement now; added savour.

Rebecca, a sprinter, streaked ahead, running in a straight line for the island, her fair hair billowing out behind her, the wind stinging her cheeks and rushing down the front of her tracksuit which was open at the neck.

'Isn't this glorious!' she cried.

Halfway across Tish drew level with her and now their shoes made noisy sucking noises in the wet sand with its eddying puddles where the sea had been so briefly before. Sue was only a little way behind.

'Running where nobody's run before!' shouted Tish above the wind, her black curly hair almost standing on end. 'We're nearly there!'

She spurted on then, leaving Rebecca and Sue behind, and was the first to reach the island. Soon the three of them were scrabbling up the steep sandy banks of the uninhabited lump of land, wild and scrubby with a few bent trees and the derelict cottage sitting on the top of it. 'Quick!' laughed Rebecca in excitement. 'Let's go straight up and explore the artist's house. We've got about ten minutes, haven't we?'

They were on Mulberry Island. This was wonderful fun!

And none of them heard the faint voice, far behind them in the distance, carried away on the wind:

'Wait for me! Oh, wait for me!'

'There's a huge great iron bedstead up here!' Rebecca cried out in wonderment. She had climbed up the rickety staircase to explore, leaving the other two still down below. 'He left his bed behind. And a bookcase with some books still in it, all covered in cobwebs – and there's a swallow's nest. Inside the room!' She cupped her hands to her mouth and called down. 'Quick, you *must* come and look.'

'We've found a tin of biscuits. It's never been

opened!' That was Tish's voice, shouting up the stairs. 'But we can't hang around, you know. Come on, Rebeck. Time to get back now.'

'Oh, all right then,' said Rebecca, with great reluctance.

She stepped over to the window, to take one quick look through it. There was no glass in the window and she was able to lean out. What a lovely outlook the man had had from here – straight across to the mainland, with a beautiful view of Mulberry Castle, high above the cove . . .

'Rebecca!' cried a faint little voice.

Dropping her eyes from the distant castle to

the expanse of wet sand they'd just traversed a few minutes earlier, Rebecca went rigid.

It was an alarming sight!

A small figure was coming this way, very slowly indeed, limping painfully and clutching her side.

'Holly Thomas!' she gasped.

She thundered down the stairs and shouted to the other two:

'Holly followed us; I've just seen her. She's almost here!'

Sue went pale. Tish groaned.

The three of them rushed down the steep path, overgrown with weeds and brambles, that led from above and then half scrambled, half fell down the steep bank that dropped down to flat sand below.

'Holly!'

She was sitting on a slab of rock, clutching her side. Her face was creased up with pain, but through the pain she was shining-eyed, triumphant.

'I made it. See, I made it! I'll just have a bit of a rest, I've got a stitch, and then I'm going up there to look at that house –' She pointed. 'Wouldn't it make a lovely secret den?'

'Holly!' Sue ran across to her. 'You stupid idiot. What did you follow us for? You can't look at anything, there isn't time!'

'You can't even have a rest,' said Tish, curtly. She was glancing at her watch. 'Come on, up you get.' She and Sue together, one on each side, helped Holly on her feet. 'We've got to *run*!'

They bundled her along between them. She was limping and very slow, still clutching her side. 'I only want a little rest, Tish –'

Rebecca brought up the rear. They were going hardly faster than walking pace. She scanned the sand ahead of them; she could see a tongue of sea creeping forward, trying to join up with a tongue of water on the other side.

'Why *can't* I have a rest?'

'Because the tide's just about to turn, that's why. Now shut up!'

'It's turned!' cried Rebecca then.

They all saw it at once – and heard it. Whooosh!

The first tongue of sea raced across the sands ahead of them, followed by another and then another. It all happened very quickly.

'Lift Holly on my back, Sue – hurry!' shouted Tish. 'I think we can still make it. We've got to move a lot faster than this, though. And we're going to get our feet wet, too.'

'We're going to get more than our feet wet,' said Sue. Holly was suddenly tearful and looking scared, scrambling hastily up on to Tish's back. 'What do you think, Rebecca?'

'How can we tell?' said Rebecca, staring at that ribbon of water that now separated them from the mainland.

'Okay, Holly?' said Tish edgily. 'Right, let's go if we're going, shall we?'

SIX
Two Very Angry People

By eight o'clock that evening Margot, Elf and Mara were feeling sick with worry and so were the rest of the Fourth Years in Court House. So was the Principal of Trebizon School.

'What on earth should we do now, George?' asked Miss Welbeck, at her home in the school grounds. 'Should we inform the police?'

Colonel George Peters, a very dear friend of hers who lived in the town and a school governor, had come straight over to see her, as he always did in moments of crisis. Miss Morgan was there, too. She had spent the past hour driving round the town and up and down the top road, searching for some sign of the missing girls.

'I've been to Fenners – all the usual haunts –

but nobody's seen them,' said the Juniper House Mistress, looking pale and distraught. 'They were *definitely* going to the town. I gave them strict instructions not to let Holly go any further than the main gates, but clearly they disobeyed me – and the four of them must still be together, wherever they are. Somewhere in the town, presumably! But where?'

'And there's no chance that they could have come back by way of the beach and got into difficulties, trapped in a cave, perhaps?' queried Colonel Peters.

'There's no sign of them at all there. There's no sign of anybody,' replied Miss Welbeck. Not only her own prefects, but a party of senior boys from Garth College, some brothers of the missing girls amongst them, had scoured the beaches between the school and the town, even going into the caves in Mulberry Cove and shouting and calling. 'Harry says none of our girls has been in the bay since about four o'clock this afternoon. It's been such a windy, dismal day.'

Harry was the school's lifeguard.

'And there are no boats or surfboards missing?'

'Definitely not, George.' Miss Welbeck shivered. 'I'm glad to say. And there's no possibility at all that they would have gone for a swim on their way back. Not in this cold, windy weather.'

Colonel Peters walked across to the window of the Principal's sitting room and stared out into her garden. 'It's late,' he mused. 'Very nearly dark.' He swung round to face Miss Morgan. 'The little one's got a gammy leg, you say? Could have found it hard slog then? Might have had difficulty making it back?'

Miss Morgan nodded.

'Then it seems to me somebody might have stopped and offered them a lift,' he said. 'It would have been as they were coming along the top road, on their way *back* from the town. Because if the little 'un had been in difficulty on the way *there*, they'd just have turned back straight away. If they *were* picked up, the vehicle would have been travelling in the Clifford direction. It's only a possibility, Madeleine, but it's one we have to allow for.'

'I'd better ring the police, hadn't I?' said Miss Welbeck.

'I'm afraid so, Madeleine.'

While Elf, Margot and Mara sat huddled together, keeping a tense and silent vigil, listening for the slightest sound that might herald the return of their friends to Court House, the brothers of the missing girls at Garth College were making endless cups of coffee in the kitchen at Syon House.

Robbie Anderson, Justin Thomas and Edward Murdoch had searched the town after helping to search the beaches and had now returned exhausted. They were frantic with worry about their sisters – and not just their sisters, either. David Murdoch was away on a school trip and so missed it all.

Justin, the most sensitive – and the most imaginative – of the three of them, was pale and trembling by this time.

'Cheer up, Justy,' said Robbie. 'Nobody could possibly have kidnapped them. Not four of them. Not if you knew my sister! It'll be some kind of crazy prank, just you wait and see.'

But secretly Robbie was resolving to be up at first light, to check those caves in the cliffs at the back of Mulberry Cove again. They'd already checked them once, but at least it would be something to do.

'I thought Sue was the responsible kind,' said Justin bitterly.

Colonel Peters had taken charge of the situation and when Miss Welbeck's phone rang, very late that evening, he took the call. He was hoping that it would be the police with some news by now.

But it was a young reporter from the local newspaper.

'Good evening,' he said in a pleasant voice. 'Mrs Tarkus has just telephoned me and said there are some Trebizon girls missing and I wondered if Miss Welbeck would be kind enough to make a statement –?'

Under his breath, Colonel Peters cursed that local lady, a busybody who disapproved of modern youth and was always stirring up trouble for the local schools, which did admittedly rather dominate the town at times.

'Oh, dear, not Mrs Tarkus again?' he said, pretending to laugh. Then, in a level tone: 'Look here, my good man, these are not Miss Welbeck's working hours and right now she is entertaining friends to drinks. If you have anything important to discuss with her, I suggest you phone her at her office tomorrow, during school hours.'

'Yes, sir. Of – of course,' said the reporter, disconcerted.

Colonel Peters replaced the phone and walked through to the sitting room to rejoin Miss Welbeck and Miss Evelyn Gates, the Senior mistress at Trebizon.

'I'm afraid Mrs Tarkus has been busy already,' he said, mopping his brow. 'That was the press. I've managed to put them off – for the moment.'

'The police. Now the press,' said Miss Welbeck. She looked grey with worry. 'And still no news of the girls.'

'With Ishbel Anderson involved,' said Miss Gates drily, 'I can't help feeing in my *bones* that some high jinks lie at the back of it all.'

'If that proves to be the case and the school's reputation were to be damaged because of it,' said the Principal, slowly and thoughtfully, 'then I would find it very difficult to forgive those responsible.'

'In the meantime,' said the colonel, 'I've told the press that you're entertaining friends to drinks. So how about pouring me a scotch, Madeleine, dear? I could certainly do with one.'

'Ooh, isn't this fun?' giggled Holly, from the floor. It was pitch dark in the bedroom of the old cottage. 'I'm really cosy and warm. And I'm not a bit scared. Didn't I say this would make a good den?'

'Oh, do shut up!'

'For goodness' sake let's all try and get some sleep!'

'We've got to get up early, remember?' said Tish, tersely. 'Like dawn, for instance. We're not exactly supposed to *be* here.'

She shivered. They'd made Holly a bed on the floor with some old cushions and found a moth-eaten carpet to cover her with, so that she'd be warm and comfortable for the night. But poor them – they had to make do with being huddled together on the big iron bedstead with only a couple of torn curtains they'd found for covering. And the wind was blasting in off the sea straight through the window frame that hadn't any glass in it, the one where Rebecca had leaned out to admire the view.

Even fully dressed in their tracksuits they were cold. But it wasn't just the cold that kept them awake for a long time after Holly had gone to sleep: it was worry and suspense as well.

'All murder is going to be let loose when they find us,' said Tish, miserably. 'We *could* have made it back – I know we could.'

'Don't be so sure about that,' said Sue.

It was Sue who had made Tish come back. Tish had set off at a gallop with Holly on her back and

Sue had hung back, with Rebecca hovering between the two, not quite knowing *what* to do. Then suddenly Sue had raced past Rebecca and caught up with Tish and grabbed her by the arm, jerking her to a halt.

'No, Tish! If it were just us three we'd make it easily, but we can't chance it. Not with Holly. We don't know how deep that water's going to be by the time we get there –'

They'd stood there arguing furiously and then –

'Look, the whole thing's decided,' Rebecca had

said, pointing. The water was gradually spreading. 'Even if we could have made it, I don't think we can risk it now. Come on, let's go back to the cottage.'

Later, from their vantage point on top of the island, they'd actually seen the search party in Mulberry Cove, just tiny distant figures, and had shouted and waved and tried to attract their attention. But the light was poor and the wind so loud it had drowned their faint cries. They'd watched helplessly as the search party had left the cove. They were stranded for the night!

And with no electricity, no torches, not even a box of matches – and darkness fast approaching – they'd got the beds organised, demolished the tin of biscuits between them and settled down for the night.

'I *know* we could have made it,' Tish was insisting. 'It wasn't very far. A hundred to one, we would have made it.'

'It's the *one* that worried me,' Sue retorted.

'*Please* stop arguing you two,' pleaded Rebecca. 'Let's try and get some sleep.'

It was dawn when she awoke. She was the first to wake up.

A beautiful dawn; the wind had dropped and

the birds were singing and the sky was streaked with pink and purple. Nothing seemed quite so bad now.

Rebecca tiptoed to the window, taking with her the ragged curtain that had been her bedcover, intending to hang it out as a signal to the mainland. She stared across the shimmering sea to the cove. The tide was low again but not low *enough*. Spring tides, that was all.

Suddenly she realised that somebody was moving about over there.

Leaning out of the window, she waved the curtain frantically and cried '*Help!*', startling the others in the room into immediate wakefulness.

Some sixth sense, or was it the slight movement seen out of the corner of the eye, made the boy in the cove turn full face to the island. Somebody was in the cottage there! There was something fluttering at an upstairs window.

Found them! he thought in relief. Found them!

It was Robbie Anderson.

And in less than half an hour he had them taken off the island by motor boat, his arm tightly round Rebecca's shoulders all the way back, much too overjoyed to utter one word of criticism against any of them.

Not so Miss Welbeck. She was in a grim mood when she called the three friends to her study before morning school. They had showered and changed and Mrs Barrington had cooked them a huge breakfast over at Court House, heartily relieved to see them back safe and well. But now came the moment of reckoning.

'You have wasted the police's time. You have had a lot of people up half the night and extremely worried about you. You have let me down and you have let Trebizon down. Only by a hair's breadth have I managed to keep this incident out of the newspapers,' Miss Welbeck added. 'By sheer good fortune you were back at school this morning by the time local press and radio contacted me, and I was able to inform them, perfectly truthfully, that there were no girls missing from Trebizon and that if they wanted a sensational story they had better look elsewhere.'

She surveyed them coldly.

'It's no use pleading extenuating circumstances. Certainly Holly Thomas had no right to break bounds and leave the main gates and follow you but it was also *your* responsibility to see that didn't happen. Doubly so in view of the quite outrageous

73

things you were planning to do. As for breaking bounds yourselves and going to the island without permission – deliberately deceiving Miss Morgan in order to do so – it leaves me speechless. It was the height of folly and you know it. You are allowed a great deal of freedom here and you are not expected to abuse it. You have betrayed my trust and you have come near to hurting the school.'

She rose to her feet, signalling that the interview was almost at an end. She walked across to the window of her study and gazed out at the rolling parkland that lay to the front of the school, with its old oaks and grassy knolls. A herd of deer grazed in the distance.

'It can take a hundred years to build up a fine reputation for a school,' she said, standing with her back to them. 'It can be destroyed almost overnight. I hope you will remember that in future.'

Very curtly, without even turning round, she said:

'That's all. Except to say, I'm surprised. From you three, I expected better. You are dismissed.'

They walked back to Court House together to get ready for lessons, feeling miserable.

'Phew,' said Tish.

Later that day, when they heard that Holly had been given a detention, Mara said: 'Why, you lucky things, you didn't even get a punishment!'

Tish replied: 'Oh yes we did.'

'I'd rather have had a detention any time,' said Rebecca.

She would have preferred almost anything to Miss Welbeck's cold and quite justifiable anger.

Somebody else was very angry. Justin Thomas.

He wrote Sue a short letter saying that while he appreciated her kindness in taking Holly under her wing, not to bother in future. Also he wouldn't be able to make it at the weekend, after all, as he had a lot of work to catch up on.

The letter arrived on the Saturday morning and Sue took it very badly.

'None of this would have happened if we'd run like mad and beat the tide,' Tish said stubbornly to Rebecca.

'We'll never know, will we?' said Rebecca.

Anyway, that was only one way of looking at things.

SEVEN
Edging Forward

As time passed, Miss Welbeck went out of her way – with a word of praise here, a smile there – to show that she'd forgiven the three friends for their lapse. On this one occasion they'd gone too far, much too far, and there could have been very serious repercussions – but it was all over now, safely behind them.

Before the incident was completely forgotten, she had one anxious moment. Miss Gates brought to her the current edition of The *Juniper Journal*, a little news sheet that the juniors produced once a week on an old duplicating machine (actually donated by Mara's father when 'the six' had themselves been juniors: in fact The *J.J.* had been founded by Tish Anderson in Rebecca's first term at Trebizon). It had been sold round the Staff Room, as usual, and Miss Gates had been slightly alarmed to see that Holly Thomas had written up her adventure as the lead story under the headline 'My Night on Mulberry Island.'

'Three Fourth Years have been letting me do training with them and last Thursday we decided to run to Mulberry Island because the tide was right out. (Nobody must ever try to do this again because it is very dangerous.) Anyway, what happened was this, we got cut off by the tide and we went in the empty house there and . . .'

Glancing at the story, Miss Welbeck pursed her lips.

'Putting rather a gloss on things, isn't she? Giving the impression that she went to the island at the personal invitation of the older girls! I don't believe that for one moment.'

'Quite so,' agreed the Senior mistress. 'She tagged along in secret and not wanted. But she's hardly going to put that in the story. In any case, she's probably genuinely forgotten such a small detail in all the excitement of being regarded as a heroine by the rest of the junior school! Well, Madeleine, what do you want me to do about these newsletters?'

'Have them all rounded up and destroyed,' said Miss Welbeck.

'What reason shall we give for the confiscation?'

'That Holly's story sets a very bad example and is nothing to boast about,' retorted the Principal. 'And for good measure,' she added, 'tell Miss Morgan to tell the editor that publication of The *J.J.* is to be suspended for two weeks, as a mark of my displeasure.'

It was done.

But at least one copy of the offending newsletter escaped. Holly had posted a copy to her brother at Garth, hot off the press, with a note scribbled at the bottom saying:

I thought you'd like to read this, Justy. I'm nearly as famous as Della now.

He wrote a disapproving letter back, pointing out that Della would not have done anything so stupid. He noted to himself that Holly's version of events differed slightly from the one Robbie Anderson had given him. He didn't know which to believe but, either way, the newsletter made him feel angry with Sue Murdoch all over again.

He had really liked Murdoch's sister and he'd thought there seemed something trustworthy about her. But her promise to take Holly under her wing had led to his getting the biggest fright of his life!

After Laura, he should have known better. All girls thought about was having fun. You couldn't really depend on them.

Sue was very hurt and upset by Justin's attitude – and after that she kept out of Holly's way. Holly didn't *need* looking after any more, anyway! As Miss Gates had observed, she'd shot to fame since the Mulberry Island adventure. After a very difficult first year, Holly Thomas was now somebody in her own right and no longer lived in the shadow of the older sister who'd been such an illustrious pupil at Trebizon. In fact it was the pathetic boasting about Della that had prompted the name-calling from Sarah Butters and Co., but that was all in the past now.

By the time Junior Charity Week arrived, in early May, Holly was cheered round the athletics track by quite a large crowd of girls and managed, gasping and determined, to complete four whole laps.

'Didn't I do well, Sue?' said Holly, flushed and shining-eyed when she came over to Court House to collect her sponsorship money. 'I'm afraid that's forty pence you owe me – you as well, Rebecca!'

Mara owed quite a lot more than that.

After the girl had gone, noting Sue's chastened look, Mara said:

'Life is not at all fair! Holly is so happy now and it is all thanks to you, Susan. And Tish and Rebecca, of course. But did you get any thanks from Justin? No!'

'Oh, let's forget about it,' said Sue quickly.

But Rebecca agreed with Mara. Life was monstrously unfair. Poor Sue. She was still eating her heart out about Justin Thomas, Rebecca could tell. She would just have to try and get over him.

Tish's craze for running continued as strongly as ever but Sue and Rebecca dropped out of the training runs in time. Sue first, saying that she had too much music practice, but probably because the idea had lost its savour for her. Then Rebecca.

As Rebecca's tennis programme for the term got under way she realised that this would be more than enough to keep her fit! There just weren't enough hours in the day to go running as well. Apart from school matches and regular team practices, there were county fixtures, sessions with Mrs Ericson, her professional coach at Exonford, and two major tournaments during May.

And there were the early morning practice sessions, as well. They soon became a regular thing. While Tish was out running, Rebecca would be out on the grass courts with Joss Vining or Trisha Martyn or Miss Darling, the tennis teacher, hitting the ball backwards and forwards, backwards and forwards.

'Let's have a proper game,' she would say to Joss occasionally.

But Joss would reply: 'Oh, Rebecca, there isn't time. Let's concentrate on our strokes on grass. My backhand's getting more and more erratic, if you ask me, and you'd better do something about that smash of yours if you want to get to Eastbourne.' Or words to that effect.

And of course that was only sensible.

But frustrating.

All this hectic tennis was a bit much for Rebecca sometimes. She would like to have done more swimming and surfing. The weather was getting sunny and warm. Elf and Margot, particularly, were spending a lot of time in the sea. She was sad not to join Gardening Club this term, but there wasn't any point if she wasn't going to have enough time to do any gardening. Occasionally, when the weather was too wet for tennis practice, she went to Cookery Club with Elf and Sue. That was good fun.

She was falling behind with school work. The long light evenings were to blame; she was always needed out on the tennis courts and she skipped through her prep much faster than she should, except for GCSE coursework assignments.

Towards half-term, the Fifth Year girls in Court became noticeably subdued, revising up on the top floor in their study cubicles for hours on end, their GCSEs almost upon them. Nobody looked more subdued than Margaret Exton. Passing her on the stairs one day, Rebecca felt that same little jolt that she'd experienced on the first day of term.

'Mum and Dad are coming to see Miss Welbeck at the end of term' Rebecca remembered. 'Oh dear, I must do some work soon.'

But the very next day, Mr Pargiter said to her, in the Latin lesson:

'No, Rebecca, the word microscope comes from

the Greek – *mikros*, little and *skopein*, to look at. We'll be doing some Greek together in the Sixth Form.'

Afterwards, Rebecca whispered to Tish:

'Did you hear what he said? About Greek in the Sixth Form?'

'What about it?' asked Tish, puzzled to notice how flushed and pleased Rebecca was looking.

'In the *Sixth Form*,' said Rebecca.

'I'll be doing all science by then!' grinned Tish.

Tish wanted to be a doctor, like her father, and was learning Latin simply to help her with all the medical terms, later on. But she enjoyed the lessons.

'Still, I expect it'll be good,' added Tish.

'Yes, really good,' murmured Rebecca.

She let the matter drop. She couldn't be bothered to explain that it was not so much the mention of Greek as the mention of the Sixth Form that had excited her. Mr Pargiter just seemed to take it for granted somehow that Rebecca would be staying on after the Fifth next year. A continuing relationship, stretching on happily into the future, stretching on and on, with no clouds on the horizon . . .

Rebecca sighed happily and stared dreamily out of the window, feeling as though a little weight had been lifted from her shoulders.

Officially athletics ended with Sports Day, at half-term, but Tish was overjoyed when Angela Hessel offered to continue to coach her in the 1500 metres beyond then.

'You're doing very well at the distance,' she told her. 'I want you to get some more competition. There are two meetings you can go to, after half-term, and if you do well there, I think you'll be accepted for the West of England meeting at the end of June.'

Tish broke the school record in the intermediate 800 metres on Sports Day – there was no 1500 metres event – and Laura Wilkins and Aba Amori both had a good day, too, breaking records for the 100 metres and 200 metres respectively.

Joss Vining, who would have won the long jump with ease, was absent at a territorial summer hockey tournament for players under twenty-one. She had not been able to attend one Athletics Club meeting this term. On top of all her tennis, the bigwigs in women's hockey were suddenly taking a close interest in her, and had invited her to this tournament. It was a very great honour, but her happiness was clouded somewhat by her father's attitude. The future he had in mind for her lay with tennis, not hockey.

Rebecca was also absent from Sports Day, having been taken to a tennis tournament up north by her county coach, an important one. They stayed in a hotel – a proper hotel! – for Rebecca was now beginning to earn a modest amount of money from her tennis, which just about covered expenses. On this occasion Rebecca won a hundred pounds for reaching the semi-finals, but it was the result more than the money that Mrs Ericson was pleased about.

'This will look good on your entry!' she said.

She was thinking of course about the British Junior Grasscourt Championships at Eastbourne. In August. Rebecca had been sent the entry form at the beginning of April – but it didn't have to be in until the second of July. She would have to enter her twelve best wins on the form and six other commendable results.

From the tournament Rebecca went straight on down to Gloucestershire to spend half-term with her grandmother. Mrs Ericson drove her most of the way.

'Do you know, I still haven't played a match against Joss Vining since she came home from America?' she confided, during the long drive. In the tournament just past, Rebecca had been beaten in the semi-finals by the current Under-16 number one in Britain – a girl with whom Joss had always been neck and neck.

'Oh, won't Joss play you? What a spoilsport,' laughed Mrs Ericson. She kept her eyes on the road ahead. They were whipping along, very fast. 'Don't you have a school tournament?'

'No. Isn't that odd!' realised Rebecca.

'Well, don't worry,' said the coach. 'It's the county junior closed tournament next month. You'll be in the two opposite halves of the draw so, unless there's some very surprising upset, you and Joss will meet in the final.'

'The county closed?' exclaimed Rebecca.

Of course!

Rebecca's eyes sparkled as she watched the countryside slip by. It was a bright day, with not much cloud around; big patches of blue sky, green fields, trees out in full leaf everywhere. The end of May in England, what a lovely time of year it was! She recalled that the Nathan twins, who were in IV Alpha with her, had their birthday on the thirtieth of May. 'And do you know, Rebecca, it never rains on our birthday; it's always sunny,' Ruth Nathan had once told her. 'That's a fact.' Rebecca loved useless facts.

But she spent most of half-term indoors, working furiously in the peace and quiet of the bungalow, while her grandmother fussed round her with cups of tea and chocolate biscuits. It was a heaven-sent opportunity to catch up on French, German and Latin learning and read through her English set books. The best chance of pleasing her parents, Rebecca had decided, was to shine in her favourite subjects in the end-of-term exams – and hope they'd turn a blind eye to the rest.

And in the meantime, Mrs Ericson seemed certain that she'd get her match with Joss Vining at last. In the final of the county closed!

Rebecca never dreamt how important that match was going to be . . .

And a famous match in every sense of the word.

Because it was during that half-term holiday, while Rebecca was immersed in French verbs at her grandmother's, that the film company telephoned Miss Welbeck.

EIGHT
The Mysterious Miss Angel

'A film is going to be made about Trebizon,' Miss Welbeck announced to the school in Assembly, one morning.

A ripple of excited whispers at once ran round and round the hall.

It was a Friday morning in the latter half of June.

The film company concerned was a small one called Silent Eye Productions Ltd that specialised in documentary films about contemporary life as it really was – the 'fly on the wall' kind of film – and they had persuaded a television company that life in and around a famous boarding school would be an excellent subject for British viewers. From a shortlist of schools they had made Trebizon their first choice, apparently because of its spectacular setting by the sea and the fact that it was such a well-known school.

'We shall, of course, be even more well known after this,' Miss Welbeck told the assembled girls, with a smile. 'This is quite an honour. The film unit arrives in the town this weekend. They have booked into the Trebizon Bay Hotel and will be filming around school all next week – right up to Commemoration Day next Saturday. It's a small unit, just two cameramen, one technician, the film director and his personal assistant. They assure me that they will be very unobtrusive, for that is the way they work, and disruption to school life will be minimal.'

Since that first phone call at half-term there had been letters exchanged between the film company and the school, the proposals had been cleared by the Governors and agreement reached. But it had been a well kept secret, Miss Welbeck holding back the announcement until the last moment in order not to stir up too much excitement, especially amongst the junior girls. She had selected the coming week because school exams would still be a whole fortnight away, the Fifth and Upper Sixth forms would be far too busily occupied finishing their public examinations to concern themselves with the fact that a film was being made, and the Commem celebrations would, she hoped, make a fitting climax to the week's filming.

'You will notice the cameras around,' she told the assembled school, 'but it is most important that you ignore them completely. Just carry on with your daily round as though they were *not there*.'

The film company had sent Miss Welbeck a video of one of their prize winning documentaries, *A Day in the Life of a Miner*, and both she and the Governors had been impressed by its air of factual reportage and quiet authenticity. 'There is to be no silliness or showing off, of any kind. Nor do you have to be on your best behaviour. Just be your natural selves, that is all that is required.'

Miss Welbeck had a final announcement to make.

'I am asked by Miss Willis to point out that there is a large collection of odd, unmarked games socks over at the sports centre and would the owners please come and claim them . . .'

But nobody was listening.

A film company was arriving in the town this weekend. They were going to make a film about Trebizon!

Rebecca saw two of the film people in the town on the Saturday afternoon, when she met Robbie for a cup of coffee at Fenners. She'd noticed the big white van parked outside the Trebizon Bay Hotel, when she'd cycled into town, with the name *Silent Eye Productions Ltd* painted on the side of the van.

'They're going to make a film about Trebizon, Robbie!' Rebecca told him, excitedly.

'They look like typical film people, don't they?' he grinned. 'Just how they're supposed to look.'

It was true. From their vantage point in a window seat at Fenners, they could see the pair on the opposite side of the street – a cameraman taking some establishing shots of the picturesque town with a hand-held camera, a young woman at his side making notes on a large pad. Both wore white tee shirts with the company name *Silent Eye* and a bright green unblinking eye die-stamped across the back of the shirts. The cameraman, who was quite young but already balding, wore an eye-shade against the sun. The young woman, whom Rebecca presumed was the PA to the director that Miss Welbeck had mentioned, was the epitome of glamour and elegance. She had piles of blonde hair framing her face, the biggest pair of sunglasses that Rebecca had

ever seen, fluorescent make-up on her face and an exceptionally perfect figure which enabled her to get away with wearing some brilliant pink jeans, very tight, that others might have thought twice about.

'Isn't *she* just something?' laughed Rebecca.

'Extraordinary,' said Robbie. 'She doesn't look real, somehow! She looks as though she's in films herself, not just helping to make them. You don't know her name by any chance?'

Rebecca had seen their names up on the school noticeboard.

'Miss Angel,' she replied.

'Glamorous!' he exclaimed. And they both laughed.

But Robbie and Rebecca, snatching a rare meeting during this hectic term, had something more important to discuss. They'd met up this afternoon to talk about the county closed.

It would take place at Exonford over two days next week – the Thursday and the Friday.

'I've got triple maths and an Oxbridge class next Thursday,' Robbie told her, 'but I've managed to dodge a few things Friday, so I'm coming! If Mrs Barry gives her permission, I can take you there in the car and bring you back afterwards.'

'Oh, Robbie, that's wonderful!' said Rebecca.

'So make sure you don't get knocked out on the first day, Rebeck. Not when I've gone to so much trouble.'

'I *can't* get knocked out!' Rebecca wailed. 'I'm going to reach the final and play Joss Vining if it kills me.'

Robbie smiled; he'd been joking. He knew what a significant match this was going to be for Rebecca

– much more significant than Rebecca had realised when Mrs Ericson had first mentioned it at half-term.

'Let's have some cream cakes on that,' he said, signalling to the waitress to come over. He looked at Rebecca thoughtfully. 'And don't forget to bring Biffy with you on Friday, either.' Biffy was their lucky mascot bear.

'I'll bring Biffy all right,' said Rebecca, with feeling.

She was exceptionally keyed up now about the county closed.

There was every reason to be.

'I'm a film star!' exclaimed Tish, bursting into the big room that they all shared in Court House, at eight o'clock on Monday morning. The others were only just getting dressed and even Rebecca had slept in for once. But Tish, wearing athletics briefs and tee shirt, had already been to Mulberry Cove and back, pounding along the sands in bare feet. The mornings were very warm now.

'What are you *talking* about?' inquired Mara, yawning as she zipped up her school skirt. 'Hurry up and get changed, Tish, or we'll be late for breakfast.'

'They were over in the cove, the film people!' chortled Tish, scrabbling around in the cupboard for her school clothes. 'They were sitting on a rock down there, two of them. They took miles of film of me running across the cove and back, I saw them. Of course, I didn't take any notice, pretended they weren't there and all the rest of it. Obeyed orders!'

'Oh, Tish!' said Elf, emerging from the other room. 'What fun!'

'Down in the cove at seven thirty in the morning?' exclaimed Rebecca. 'I must say they don't hang about, do they?'

'I expect Miss Willis has told them about Tish,' pronounced Sue, just returning from the bathroom, where she'd been scrubbing her face with some special soap that was supposed to do her complexion good. 'There's bound to have been a briefing. I expect Miss Willis told them that Tish is going to be a great runner. They must have been lying in wait for you, Tish!'

'It *would* make a good scene for the film, wouldn't it?' murmured Rebecca, thinking about it. 'I mean, it's lovely down there in the early morning just now. A June morning ... the empty sands ... a solitary figure ...'

But at breakfast time, Mrs Barrington was less romantic and more realistic about it.

'I shouldn't get too excited, Tish. These fly-on-the-wall people shoot miles and miles of film. Then they take it all back to London to edit it and about three-quarters of it ends up on the cutting-room floor.'

'It's funny, Rebeck, but there's something bothering me a bit,' Tish confided in her later. 'It's been coming back to me off and on all morning. And I've just seen her again, chatting to some juniors over by the sports centre. The glamorous girl with the piles of blonde hair, Miss Angel or whatever she's called . . .'

'What about her?' queried Rebecca. They were walking towards the dining hall together and she was actually wondering what was for lunch. 'I mean, why does she bother you then?'

Tish frowned.

'There's something mysterious about her.'

'Not very real looking?' suggested Rebecca. 'That's what Robbie said.'

But Tish just shook her head. 'Oh, no, not that. She's made up to the nines, of course, but I expect they all are in film circles. No, it's silly. I just have this funny feeling that I know her and that she knows me. The way she was watching me through her dark glasses, somehow, when I was out running this morning. It sort of gave me a little shivery feeling. I definitely feel that we know each other. And yet . . .'

Tish pushed a hand through her dark curls, shook her head again and then laughed at herself.

'And yet I've never seen her before in my life, have I, Rebecca?'

'I wouldn't have thought so, Tish!' smiled Rebecca. She pushed open the glass doors into the dining hall and smelt the delicious smell of fish and chips. 'Cheer up. I expect they just cultivate that certain look ... to go with their kind of film productions.'

'What certain look?'

Rebecca, pretending to be ghostly, whispered: '*The Silent Eye*, of course.'

NINE
Filming Continues

Rebecca had discovered the significance of the county closed tournament around about the middle of June. It had come as a very great surprise to her.

The conversation with Joss Vining had come as a shock!

Both girls had filled in all their results on special forms provided and submitted them to the Lawn Tennis Association for their LTA ranking to be updated. These had to be in by the twelfth of June and, after the computer had done its work, they knew they could then expect to receive their new rankings early in July.

'You've done very well so far, Rebecca, but you won't yet have reached the top thirty-two in your age group!' Mrs Ericson had informed her. 'If you had, you'd be almost certain to be accepted for Eastbourne. But of course they accept forty-eight entries in total and I believe you stand a chance of being amongst those sixteen acceptances that don't come off the computer.'

After taking the top thirty-two off the computer, it appeared that the selectors took all sorts of other factors into consideration when picking a further sixteen girls to bring the entry up to its full forty-eight. Sometimes players had not entered important tournaments which scored high under the computer ranking rules – but in official LTA fixtures, such as county matches, had one or two notable victories which the selectors could not ignore. Or they might be previously top ranking players who'd lost form through illness or injury, only to find it again in the nick of time.

So in selecting the field for Eastbourne it was the best results right up to July second, the closing date for entry forms, that mattered – not by any means just the summer rankings, which would by then be to hand but were not regarded as infallible.

Around about the middle of June, coming back in the school minibus from an away match (where Rebecca and Joss had enjoyed a very exciting doubles victory against Helenbury's first pair), Joss was a little more relaxed and talkative than usual.

Rebecca had long given up asking Joss for a match, but now – in a roundabout way – the other girl raised it herself.

'I gather you took the champion to three sets at half-term,' she said, giving Rebecca a sidelong glance. Joss usually sat in the single seat behind the driver on these journeys but on this occasion Trisha Martyn had grabbed it; she was in the middle of exams and wanted to read through her A level history notes. So Joss was sitting next to Rebecca, at the back. 'That must have felt good.'

'It did,' said Rebecca.

'Look, Rebecca, I'm sorry we haven't had a proper match yet,' said Joss. 'But it doesn't seem worth it now. It's not very long till the county closed and everybody seems to think we'll meet each other in the final. It'll be played according to LTA rules and will really count for something. It's going to be *very* important, I think.'

'You mean for me? For Eastbourne?' asked Rebecca. 'If I can take *you* to three sets, too – it's going to improve my chances?'

It was then that Joss said the very surprising

thing. Smoothing her brown curly hair back at the temple with one hand, she gave a small smile:

'Important for you? I've no idea. From what I've heard, you should be okay. It's *my* chances ... As a matter of fact, I think I need to have a really good win. Hey, Rebecca, I don't think we should be discussing this, should we?'

Rebecca lay awake that night, digesting the conversation, trying to work it out.

The next morning, very early, she was out on the still-dewy grass courts with Miss Darling. It was a lovely midsummer morning. Miss Darling was sending low balls pounding down to the base line, one after the other, for Rebecca to retrieve. She needed all the practice on grass that she could get – and how she loved it! The fast surface, the streaking low balls, the freedom of movement as she sprinted and hurled herself around ... It was without a doubt Rebecca's favourite surface now.

But she *had* to know what Joss meant and afterwards she plucked up courage to ask Miss Darling.

'Joss Vining *is* definite for Eastbourne, isn't she? Surely?'

The tennis teacher, grey-haired and ramrod-

backed, rarely smiled, but now the grey eyes that met Rebecca's blue ones in a level look had a touch of humour there.

'Nothing's ever definite in tennis, Rebecca.'

'But *surely* –?'

'No, not definite. Lacking in dedication? Other things on mind? Hasn't entered many tournaments; hasn't beaten the right people always. Could be doubtful.'

Joss – doubtful! It seemed unthinkable to Rebecca. She had been playing in national tournaments since she was twelve and since then had had a whole year in the States, getting special coaching and some marvellous competition, the firm hand of her father guiding her every step of the way. And this term, in their doubles matches together, Joss had pulled out the kind of tennis on occasions which Rebecca could still only hope to aspire to.

'Well, if Joss is doubtful then – then I'm *impossible*,' said Rebecca, with sinking spirits.

'Nonsense. Perfectly possible. Quite likely. You've been beating just the right people this year, Rebecca. You should squeeze in. Unless . . .'

'Unless what?' asked Rebecca quickly.

Again, the touch of humour in the grey eyes.

'Try and work it out for yourself. If Josselyn is going to re-establish her quality in the eyes of the selectors, then she needs to get a move on. I believe she's playing Rachel Cathcart next week. After that, you two will no doubt meet in the final of the county closed.'

'And Joss doesn't just need to beat me? She needs to wipe me out?' suggested Rebecca.

'If she is to be *sure* of Eastbourne. Yes, I'm afraid so.'

'And that could damage *my* chances?'

'Of course.'

Rebecca absorbed all this, then spoke up, in a defiant voice:

'Well, it's got to happen first, hasn't it?'

No wonder she was keyed up, now that the week of the tournament had arrived.

All through the week, filming continued.

Any anxieties that Miss Welbeck might have had about school life being disrupted proved to be completely unfounded. Surprisingly so.

A lone cameraman had drifted in and out of school a few times, taking desultory footage of things like an art class in progress, girls filing out of the assembly hall, a Sixth Form tutorial in Parkinson. But that was all.

The rest of the unit seemed to spend most of their time on the beach or else back at the hotel working on the script.

By Thursday, Miss Welbeck was feeling slightly uneasy about one aspect of the filming. She called in Miss Sara Willis, head of the games staff.

'I gather they've taken miles of film of the girls swimming and using the surfboards.'

'They think it's colourful, Miss Welbeck. And of course the weather is absolutely glorious outside.'

'Yes,' frowned Miss Welbeck. 'And I realise that they'll be doing a lot of shooting indoors when it comes to Commem on Saturday. But even so, showing the girls in the sea all the time gives a slightly unbalanced picture of life here. Another thing concerns me. I specifically told them that any scenes in the bay should include Harry – but I gather from Harry that they've hardly filmed him at all. He's quite hurt about it.'

'It's not his pride I'm concerned about. This film is already slotted for a television showing and will be seen by a wide audience. If swimming scenes are included and don't finish up in the cutting room, I want viewers to be quite clear that we have a professional lifeguard on duty at all times, as well as members of staff where the younger girls are concerned. Quite apart from the fact that no girl goes into the sea until she's passed her bronze. Have they taken any film at the indoor pool?'

'Not yet,' said Miss Willis. 'But I'm sure they will! And the director's assured me we'll see rushes of the finished film, Miss Welbeck.' Sara Willis had been getting on rather well with Mark Coughlin, the man directing the film; a slim, dark-haired man, softly spoken and very charming. 'They've taken some lovely shots of Margot Lawrence surfing – very dramatic with her dark skin, white malibu board, sparkling turquoise sea – very filmic.'

'Quite so.' Miss Welbeck spoke crisply and decisively. 'Nevertheless, Sara, I want them deflected. They have quite enough film of Trebizon Bay. Surely there are other things happening? Can I leave it with you?'

'I know the very thing!' said Miss Willis. 'It's the county closed at the moment. Our two young tennis stars here are almost certain to be playing each other in the final tomorrow – and a coachload of girls is going to Exonford to cheer them on. I'll insist to Mr Coughlin that they go and film the whole thing.'

'At my special request, please,' nodded Miss Welbeck. She smiled and felt more relaxed. 'That's a splendid idea, Sara.'

'If the old trout's getting worried, I suppose we'd better go and cover this tennis match, then,' said Mark Coughlin to his team, down at the Trebizon

Bay Hotel on the Friday morning.

He eyed the two cameramen.

'We'll need both cameras, I guess. Get the gear packed up and put in the van. What about you, Libby? Do you want to come?'

'If I must,' sighed his personal assistant.

They drank their coffee slowly and later ambled out of the hotel to their vehicle.

<u>TEN</u>
The Big Match – and After

In less than half an hour's time, Rebecca was due to play Joss Vining in the final of the county closed tournament for junior girls aged sixteen years and under. A coachload of spectators from Trebizon had already arrived at the grass tennis courts in Exonford Park, at the back of the sports centre, having left school immediately after lunch. They were thronging round the wire netting on the far side of Number One court, where the big match was to be played, talkative groups and gaggles of juniors and a few Middle School girls – including, of course, the rest of 'the six' who'd all used their powers of persuasion to get off Friday afternoon lessons and bag seats on the coach.

'The film people are here!' said Elf, in delight.

Cameras were being set up on stands at each end of Number One court and sound recording equipment was being checked. 'They must have got permission!'

'And there's Rebeck – she's getting some practice in, with Robbie!' commented Tish, shading her eyes and staring along to Number Six court. She could see two tracksuited figures skimming balls backwards and forwards over the net down there. She shouted and waved. 'Yahoo!'

But Rebecca was too deeply engrossed to hear. She was only dimly aware of the distant hum of voices, mingled with the nearby humming of wild bees that swarmed all over the honeysuckle at the back of Number Six court, as she practised turning her racket head to put maximum top spin on the balls that Robbie was sending down to her.

'That's it, Rebeck.'

The previous day, Rebecca and Joss had travelled to Exonford together by train, then back home to Trebizon in the evening, having done what was expected of them in the earlier rounds of the tournament. On the journey back, in particular, they'd spoken very little. Partly through exhaustion, partly because there was a certain tension hanging in the air between them now.

Today, Friday, Rebecca was relieved that Mrs Barrington had allowed her to be driven to Exonford by Robbie – Joss travelling separately with her father who, taking the day off, had driven over from Clifford to pick her up at Norris House after breakfast.

Rebecca had won her quarter-final in two sets easily and then been rather more stretched by Madeleine Marks in the semi-final, though still winning in two sets, 7–6, 6–2. Joss had had rather softer competition in her quarter and semi-finals and came through easily.

'But that's no bad thing,' Robbie had said, during the long break for lunch. 'She won't be half as tuned up as you, Rebeck. That match with Madeleine was just what you needed. I've noticed something. With the grass still being slightly damp, Joss isn't handling balls with heavy top spin at all well. I was watching her earlier.'

There'd been some rain during the night. Heavily sliced balls were lethal to deal with. So that's what Rebecca was practising now; it provided a gentle limbering-up session before the big match.

After a while, Mrs Seabrook, the county tennis scout, came across.

'Time to get ready, Rebecca,' she said, tapping her watch.

Robbie walked with her as far as the pavilion.

'I'm nervous, Robbie,' she said.

'Calm down,' he said. 'Joss has got the big reputation, even if it's a bit tarnished at the moment. She'll be more nervous than you are. It's much worse for her. And the first set's going to be the worst one, as far as Joss is concerned. Give it everything you've got, try and get the upper hand in the very first game.'

He went off to the car to find Biffy and Rebecca dived into the changing rooms. Under her track suit, she was wearing a new tennis dress, with pink edging. She had a pink and white headband to match. She washed and talced and got every last wisp of hair back under the headband, gazing out of the changing room window.

She saw the film cameras over by Number One court and quite a lot of people gathered. The referee and umpire were talking to the line judges. Joss was sitting on a bench with her father, their heads together, deep in conversation.

Rebecca felt a pang of envy. How wonderful to have a father who knew so much about tennis – Mr

Vining had played at county level himself when young – who could drive you around everywhere you needed to go. Take you to the States with him, even! Her own parents didn't know the first thing about tennis. *Might you get to junior Wimbledon this year, Becky?* they'd asked her in a recent letter. What did they think she was? Only the world's top juniors got accepted there! They weren't in the least bit clued-up. Completely out-of-touch.

But they'd be proud of her if she got to Eastbourne; really proud. And they'd be home to watch her! The British Junior Grasscourts Championships were in August and they'd be home on annual leave. Oh, wouldn't that be wonderful . . .

It would be a bit more help having someone like Mr Vining for a father though, wouldn't it?

But when she walked down the pavilion steps, two tennis rackets under her arm, her five friends were waiting for her. They surrounded her, Tish waving Biffy the bear, having just grabbed him from Robbie.

'Come on Rebecca!' exclaimed Sue.

'Lots of luck!' said Mara and Elf in unison.

'You can do it – and then you'll be on television, like me!' laughed Margot.

'Come on, Rebeck.' Tish hugged her. 'You know you can do it.'

And suddenly Rebecca felt okay.

'First set to Miss Mason, six games to three. Miss Mason leads by one set to love,' said the umpire. 'Change ends please.'

As the girls towelled down and snatched drinks, on opposite sides of the umpire's chair, Mr Vining called out, rather sharply: 'Come on, Joss. Get it together.'

But Rebecca didn't even hear. Some of the juniors were calling out in piping voices: 'Well played, Rebecca!' – that was Holly Thomas, or 'Come on, Joss!' – Sarah Butters. Rebecca still heard nothing.

She was concentrating her thoughts, with pounding heart:

'I can do it, I can do it. I can beat Joss Vining. She isn't invincible. She's losing her touch! Sometimes she's brilliant, sometimes she's not. If I can keep steady, I can win, I can win.'

In the second set, Joss made a comeback. Face set, teeth gritted, she started coming into the net, sending searing volleys past Rebecca. But then

Rebecca hung back and hung in, chasing everything, retrieving everything, and took the set into a tie-break with two superb smashes.

In the tie-break, Joss's long match experience showed. She kept icy calm whereas Rebecca's nerve failed with two bad service returns.

'Second set to Miss Vining, seven games to six. One set all.'

As she walked out for the final set, Rebecca saw her friends with their faces pressed against the wire, waving to her, almost willing her to win. She noticed that Robbie had Biffy again, tucked inside his track suit top, furry face just peeping out. It suddenly made her smile. Robbie smiled back and made a thumbs up signal.

As she took up her position on the base line, ready to serve, she caught sight of Joss's agonised face.

The truth slowly dawned on Rebecca.

Robbie was right, it was much worse for Joss. She was the one who'd always had the big reputation; she was the one who had everything to lose.

To make a comeback at this stage in the season she'd needed two crushing and authoritative victories. Her match with Rachel Cathcart had been inconclusive last week. So now, to crush Rebecca had been her best hope. A year ago, when Rebecca had been such a raw new talent, that would have been a simple task.

Not any more.

And whatever Joss did in this final set, it wasn't going to make any difference. Rebecca already had twelve games to her ten. Joss *might* still be allowed to play at Eastbourne, but she had lost her chance of making it a certainty.

With the film cameras whirring the whole time, the tennis played in the final set was of a superb quality. But it was Rebecca, the more determined and confident of the two, who finally ran out the winner, nine games to seven.

'Game, set and match to Miss Mason.'

A great cheer went up as Rebecca ran to the net to take Joss's outstretched hand. What a match!

'I feel as though I've dreamt all this, Joss. I never thought this could ever happen!'

'Well, it just did, Rebecca!' Joss said. There was nothing cool about her handshake. It was respectful and genuine. She even managed a smile, too; a very rueful one. 'You were great. Thanks for a great match.'

'Cut!' said Mark Coughlin and the cameras stopped whirring.

As she came off the court and donned a tee shirt, Robbie came and swung her off her feet and kissed her. 'We'll have a bit of a party tonight, to celebrate!' he said. Then her friends surrounded her and then a crowd of juniors, wanting to clap her on the back.

They all stayed to watch Rebecca receive the cup, then had to dash off to the coach, which was waiting to take them back to Trebizon.

'Did you mean that about a party, Robbie?' asked Tish, just before she got on the coach. Rebecca was still by the courts, talking to some of the other county junior players, with Mrs Ericson hovering and waiting to speak to her.

'Of course I did,' replied Robbie. 'I'll ask old Slade when I get back. You can't come, though. You've got to get an early night.'

Tish had now had her entry accepted for the 1500 metres event at the West of England athletics meeting. She would be running in the race the following evening, the night of the Commem Ball.

'Don't be silly!' said Tish indignantly. 'It won't be that late!'

But Robbie was joking, of course.

'Bring Sue,' he said suddenly. Sue was already on the coach and out of earshot. 'And I'll make sure Justy comes. He's getting really anti-social these days. It's bad.'

The driver honked, so Robbie pushed his sister on to the coach then walked back to wait for Rebecca.

Silent Eye Productions Ltd had parked their big white van right next to Robbie's car, Rebecca noticed. She had to squeeze along the side of it in order to reach the passenger door, when the time came for Robbie to drive her back to school.

As she stood waiting for Robbie to lean across and open her door from the inside, she felt a prickly sensation down the back of her neck.

Looking round quickly she saw a heavily made-up face framed in a mass of blonde hair. The eyes behind the huge sunglasses seemed to be boring into her. There was something very hostile about the expression on the young woman's face.

Throughout the filming, Miss Angel had not been in evidence at all. But here she was, sitting behind the steering wheel of the white van, presumably waiting for the men to come and load up the film equipment. Had she been there all afternoon?

She quickly turned away as Rebecca returned her gaze.

'Come on, Rebeck!' Robbie was easing the passenger door open. 'Jump in!'

As they drove out of the car park, he said: 'Didn't know the glamorous Miss Angel was here this afternoon.'

'I got the funniest feeling just then,' said Rebecca, glancing back over her shoulder. 'I got the feeling there was something nasty about her. D'you know Tish has the feeling she's seen her somewhere before?'

'I tell you, I think she's in films herself. Maybe just plays small parts.'

'Yes, that's what Tish has decided.'

'You've probably seen her playing somebody nasty on TV.'

'Probably,' murmured Rebecca. 'I wonder?'

She wasn't quite convinced.

Sue refused to come to the party at Syon House, saying that she wanted to wash her hair.

Justin didn't appear either, remaining upstairs and telling Robbie that he had too much work to do. Neither of Sue's brothers were able to come.

It would have been a rather quiet affair if it hadn't been for Mara. She'd decided to give her white dress a try-out. The strain of saving it all term for the Commem Ball had finally proved too much. 'Put some records on,' she told Curly Watson, in the big Common Room at Syon. 'I will teach you the tango and tomorrow we will be a sensation at the Commem Ball!'

She turned round and said to the others:

'Rebecca is a film star now! Tish is a film star! Margot is a film star! Tomorrow when they see Curly and I dance the tango, perhaps they will take some film of *us*! What do you think of my dress, Robbie? Oh, I must see myself in a film wearing this dress!'

'It's sensational, Mara,' he told her.

It was, too – and soon there were boys crowding into the Common Room to watch the lovely brown-eyed Greek girl teach Curly Watson the tango. The lemonade had all gone by nine o'clock, there was much noise and laughter and all in all it was a thoroughly jolly evening.

But it wasn't quite the same, without Sue.

And Robbie was upset about Justin, too.

Rebecca and Tish were the last to go. Mrs Slade, the House Master's wife, hadn't been able to get them into the first carload back to Trebizon, so Robbie made them a cup of coffee in the kitchen while they waited for her to come back and get them. Then he went upstairs and found Justin and brought him down, tired-eyed from poring over books.

'Come and have some coffee, Just. You should have come to the party, you hermit.'

'Hallo,' smiled Rebecca. She liked Justin's rather poetic face.

'No Susan?' he inquired, glancing round the kitchen. Oddly enough, he seemed slightly disappointed.

'Well, no,' said Tish, embarrassed. 'She thought she'd wash her hair and have an early night. Good idea. That's what I should have been doing. It's my race tomorrow . . .'

But Robbie couldn't be bothered with any of that.

'Come off it, Tish. You know perfectly well Sue's upset because Justy has never forgiven her – over Holly.' He looked at the other boy. 'And it's about time you did.'

That was too much for Rebecca.

'What's Sue done that needs forgiveness?' she exclaimed.

'Agreed,' said Robbie. 'It wasn't your fault that Holly followed you that day –'

'She was never in danger!' scoffed Tish. 'Anyway – she didn't have to stay out all night! I was all prepared to run with her on my back to beat the tide. Even if the water had been a bit deep I'd have got her through –'

'Well that sounds dangerous for a start!' said Justin.

'Oh, you're as bad as Sue,' replied Tish crossly. 'It's us who –'

'What do you mean?' he asked quickly.

But Tish was in full flow.

'– it's *us* who should forgive Holly. She got us into terrible trouble.'

'What do you mean, I'm as bad as Sue?' Justin persisted.

Rebecca saw how interested he was. There was a moment's silence. Rebecca had never told anybody the full story, not even Robbie. It put Tish in a bad light, in a way. It could only come from Tish herself, couldn't it? But now, quite deliberately, she prompted her –

'It's not strictly true to say that *Holly* got us into trouble, is it?' she murmured, looking at Tish. 'I mean, Holly was quite prepared to take a chance on it, wasn't she?'

'Yes,' nodded Tish. Up to now, she'd never told anybody the full story either, because she thought it put *Sue* in a bad light. But now, looking at Justin's face, she wondered. 'It was Sue who got us into trouble, as a matter of fact.'

'Susan stopped them,' explained Rebecca.

'Physically!' said Tish ruefully. 'Wasn't prepared to take even the teeniest tiniest chance because we had Holly with us –'

Justin's face was starting to brighten.

'– I could have killed her! So that's how we ended up spending the night on the island, and giving you all a horrible fright and getting a really bad black mark on our school records. And wasting the police's time! Honestly!' Tish began to get heated as she thought about it. She turned to Rebecca and avowed, as she'd avowed before:

'None of that would have happened if we'd run like mad and beat the tide, would it, Rebeck?'

Rebecca put it into words at last.

'That's only one way of looking at things.'

'What d'you mean?' asked Tish.

Robbie had been keeping out of all this, just following the conversation very closely. But now he said –

'None of that would have happened if Susan hadn't had such a darned terrific sense of responsibility. That's the *other* way of looking at things, isn't it, Tish? That's what Rebecca means! Listen, supergirl, you should have explained all this before –'

Justin had gone rather pale.

'I got it all horribly wrong, didn't I?' he said in dismay.

At that moment Mrs Slade arrived to take the

girls back. They went outside and clambered into the car. It was midsummer, still light. But just as the car was about to drive away, Justin came rushing out and tapped on the back window. Rebecca wound it down a little way. 'What's wrong?' she asked.

'Rebecca, it's all been a misunderstanding,' he whispered. He was still looking very upset. 'Can you tell Sue that? Can you tell her I'm sorry?'

'Tell her yourself, Justy,' said Rebecca coolly, and wound the window up again.

Justin did exactly that. He phoned Sue at Court House first thing on Saturday morning.

Rebecca was still asleep, enjoying an extra rest after all the tennis, with a party on top! They weren't needed in big hall for the Commemoration celebrations until ten-thirty.

She awoke to find Sue sitting on the end of her bed, her face shining with happiness.

'Justin's asked me to forgive him! He's asked if he can take me to the Commem Ball tonight!'

'What did you say?'

'Yes, to both, of course. Oh, Rebecca, I'm in desperate trouble!' She still looked radiant as she said it. 'What *am* I going to wear?'

Rebecca yawned and stretched. 'We'll find you something.' She felt rested now and suffused with happiness. The sun was streaming into the big room. It was Commemoration Day. Justin was going to take Sue to the ball. What a triumph! She, Rebecca, had played Joss Vining at last. Played her and won. She'd waited so long for that match. But she'd never dreamt that she'd win it! Mrs Ericson said she was almost certain for Eastbourne now. Another triumph! And tonight Tish was going to run the 1500 metres at the big athletics meeting. She'd been wanting to do that all term.

As Rebecca collected her wash things and went along to have a shower, she could hear Sue singing somewhere.

'Today's going to be wonderful!' she thought.

The Mulberry Island incident was closed, at long last. They could all forget it now.

But Rebecca was quite wrong about that.

ELEVEN
Shock at the Trebizon Bay Hotel

To complete Rebecca's happiness, there was a letter from her parents waiting downstairs.

After her shower, she'd brushed her hair till it gleamed and then dressed. Commemoration Day was one of the occasions when full school uniform was required: dark royal blue skirt, long-sleeved white blouse, royal blue tie with burgundy stripe, long white socks and highly polished black shoes.

Finally Rebecca had donned her Trebizon blazer, a deep rich burgundy colour with embossed crest, the pocket edged with her tennis team colours – a single white stripe. Tish had both purple and yellow stripes along her blazer pocket, showing that she'd earned not only first team hockey colours but athletics colours as well.

In pride of place on Sue's blazer, pinned to the lapel, was the lovely brooch with the monogram *HC*, denoting that she was the Hilary Camberwell Music Scholar of her year.

'Don't we look smart?' said Rebecca, laughing, as they trooped downstairs. They'd eaten their cornflakes in the little kitchen upstairs. A lie-in and a late, light breakfast was part of the ritual of Commem Day – there would be a sumptuous buffet lunch in the dining hall later. According to Tish it was put on to impress all the visitors. According to Elf it was necessary, anyway, to revive everybody after nearly two hours of solemn music, processions and speeches.

'Smart – and very distinguished!' Mara called up from the foot of the stairs. 'That I should share a room with such distinguished people!' She then walked across to the mail board in the hall. 'Oh, lucky Rebecca! You have a letter.'

'It's from Mum and Dad!' said Rebecca, jostling past Elf and snatching the blue airmail letter from the board. 'Oh, *good*.'

As the six friends walked across the grounds to the big hall in main school, Rebecca lagged behind, reading the letter as she went. Every so often she sidestepped to dodge a car trundling visitors to Commem – local dignitaries, old girls of the school, former members of staff, or even parents who lived near enough to come. Rebecca would have liked her parents there, too, but a letter was the next best thing. It was a warm, chatty, loving letter – and they had a special request to make.

We're longing to see you at the end of term! By the way, we're STILL waiting for the Trebizon Bay Hotel to confirm our booking! Can you go down there and check with them? If there's been a slip-up and they can't have us, try the Seaview . . .

A little tremor of pleasure went through Rebecca. Only a fortnight now before her parents came home! Of course, there was the little matter of summer exams before that. She had no idea how she was going to do in *those*, but wait till they heard the news about her beating Joss Vining and winning the county closed! And Mrs Ericson seemed positive she'd get to Eastbourne now . . .

'And Mum and Dad will be home on leave all summer' thought Rebecca, joyfully. 'We'll all stay in Eastbourne together and they can come and watch me play my matches!'

She made a mental note to cycle down to the Trebizon Bay Hotel after lunch, to sort out the booking for them, as requested. Then she folded the letter up, put it in her blazer pocket and started to run.

'Hurry up, Rebeck!' Tish was calling.

Long lines of girls were forming outside the big assembly hall. The annual service in honour of Trebizon's founder was about to begin.

Someone else had received a letter that morning. Joss Vining.

It was so noteworthy that Miss Welbeck actually referred to it in the Principal's commemoration speech (which came right at the end of the morning's celebrations).

'Members of the school, past and present, continue to distinguish themselves in many different spheres,' she told the packed hall. 'I would like to add in passing a special word of congratulation to Josselyn Vining of IV Alpha. Joss is not yet sixteen – I believe her birthday is in September – but this morning she has received an invitation to join the England Under-18 hockey squad on their overseas tour in August.'

There were gasps and then loud and prolonged applause.

Afterwards, Rebecca raced to catch up with Joss in the few minutes before lunch, darting between the throngs of people who'd streamed out of the big hall, spilling on to the terraces and the school lawns, her eyes fixed on a brown curly head of hair bobbing off into the distance. Joss was striding off somewhere on her own. She looked a lonely figure, thought Rebecca. She often did.

She had to talk to her!

She caught up with her by the Hilary of all places. She was sitting on a bench, quite alone, staring at the little lake that fronted the Spanish style building that housed the music school. It was quiet here.

'Congratulations, Joss,' said Rebecca, sitting down beside her on the bench.

'Oh, hallo!' said Joss, still staring at the water. 'Thanks, Rebecca.'

'What will you do about Eastbourne now?' asked Rebecca, rather humbly. 'I mean, that's in August as well, isn't it.'

She stared at the stripes all squashed together on Joss's blazer pocket – purple, yellow, white. School colours in all three sports – phenomenal – and quite difficult to get them all on. There was something rather symbolic about that, Rebecca thought.

'I decided this morning,' said Joss. 'I'm not sending in my application form for Eastbourne. I've torn it up! I rang Daddy and told him I was going to.'

'What did he say?'

'He said that if I did that and if I accepted the invitation to go on this tour, it was up to me, but he wasn't interested. And he certainly wasn't going to bother to come to Commem this morning.'

Joss's parents lived at Clifford, only twenty miles away.

'And he hasn't come then?' said Rebecca.

'No.'

'And he usually does?'

'Always,' replied Joss. Her lip was trembling slightly and she bit it. It was the first time Rebecca had ever seen her look other than self-contained.

'Oh, Joss, I'm sorry,' she said.

'I'm not,' replied Joss. She'd recovered her composure immediately. 'I'm glad. Glad it's all over.'

She became quite talkative.

'It's the end of a dream for Daddy. It's all he's thought about for as long as I can remember – my becoming a tennis pro and going right to the top. The year in the States was all supposed to be part of the process. The only trouble was I got to play with a fantastic hockey team while I was out there and found myself looking forward to those matches more and more. Looking forward to the tennis matches less and less. As a matter of fact I *like* being part of a team – working with other people, making it all come together. It's exhilarating – it's fantastic! But if you want to be a tennis star you've got to like it out there on your own, being the centre of the stage. You need to *revel* in it! And if you don't, it doesn't matter how good you are, when you start to play the top players, their egos will smash your ego every time. I did so marvellously well from about the age of nine that I never got the chance to sit down and work out why I hated the big matches, even though I usually won them, and my father was pushing me so hard I guess I just wanted to please him all the time.

'But for months now I've been trying to explain to him. He's never listened. He just hasn't wanted to know –'

Joss folded her arms, suddenly looking very serene, all the inner conflict and tension of the past year behind her at last.

'Well, he knows *now*,' she said.

'Oh, Joss –' Rebecca was almost lost for words. 'What a thing to have to live with. What a headache.' It explained so much. It explained everything.

'It's all resolved now!' replied Joss. She smiled wryly, giving Rebecca a sidelong look. 'You helped me, you know. You helped resolve it. You're quite likely going to be the tennis star one day, not me.'

For some reason the joy that Rebecca experienced upon hearing those words was not quite as unconfined as it might once have been. They both fell silent, staring at a duck that was bobbing on the water near a huge water lily.

'And the letter this morning clinched everything?' Rebecca said, at last. 'What a triumph that is, Joss, It's marvellous! Fancy its arriving at Commem. Your father will feel *so* proud of you, when he sits down and thinks about it.'

'No he won't,' said Joss.

Rebecca got to her feet. She felt indignant.

'It's your life, Joss. Not his.'

Then she burst out:

'Nobody should be allowed to inflict their dreams on other people! We have to be allowed to have our own dreams ... don't we?'

And she hurried away, to find the others.

'Oh, Rebecca, now I shall never be a film star,' said Mara, when she got back. 'Look, they are leaving!'

The other five were amongst the big throng of people on the terrace outside the dining hall who were waiting for lunch. She'd guessed that was where she'd find them.

'TV star you mean,' said Margot. 'It's going to be a TV film.'

'TV star, film star, what does it matter,' pouted Mara. 'Whatever it is, I'm not going to be it. Oh, why are they leaving so early!'

It was true. The cameraman and sound recordist who'd been stationed at the back of the hall during the morning had packed up their equipment and were preparing to leave Trebizon. The slight dark-haired man, Mark Coughlin, the film's director, was standing at the far end of the terrace – formally shaking hands with Miss Welbeck and various members of the school's governing body – obviously saying his goodbyes.

'Apparently they've finished filming, they've got enough film now,' explained Elf. 'Miles of it. They're not staying on for the matches or the gym display or the dancing display this afternoon, or for Commem Ball tonight. They say they're in a tearing rush!'

'Oh, what a shame,' said Rebecca. 'The Ball would have made a lovely climax to the film. The hall always looks so beautiful – and the rose garden! Not to mention you in your fabulous dress of course, Mara. I'm amazed! Fancy them not staying for tonight.'

But sure enough, when they all surged into the dining hall at one o'clock, Rebecca was in time to see the white *Silent Eye* van through the opposite windows – sliding away towards the school drive with the mysterious Miss Angel at the wheel and the rest of the crew presumably on board.

Rebecca glanced at the trestle tables, groaning under the weight of the sumptuous buffet lunch that had been prepared. There were huge plates loaded with sausage rolls, cold ham, cheese straws, vol-au-vents and stacks of delicious sandwiches, all decorated with lashings of salad. And a mouth-watering display of gateaux and trifles to follow up with. She looked from that lovely food to the back of the departing van, fast disappearing down the drive.

'They didn't even stay for lunch!' she exclaimed to Margot.

She thought no more about it then, because a hand suddenly touched her arm.

'Mrs Lazarus!' exclaimed Rebecca in delight, gazing at the elderly Latin scholar whom she'd got to know the previous summer. She was one of Trebizon's oldest 'old girls'. 'How *are* you? How's Tommy?'

'I am fit – and Tommy is wonderful!' said Lottie Lazarus. She leant forward and kissed Rebecca on the cheek, then stood back and gazed at her. 'How lovely to see you again, Rebecca. You've grown. In more ways than one, I gather from Mr Pargiter.'

'Oh?' asked Rebecca in surprise.

'You've grown in mental stature, Rebecca,' said the elderly lady, her eyes twinkling. 'Mr Pargiter assures me so and I know his judgement is sound. He tells me you have linguistic gifts and that you are putting down good foundations. Oh my beloved Latin! A "dead" language so-called, but alive and well in many a word we utter! *De mortuis nil nisi bonum.*'

'Speak nothing but good of the dead?' hazarded Rebecca, shyly.

'Precisely!'

They both laughed and then Lottie Lazarus disappeared as suddenly as she'd come, tugged away into a whirlpool of people, calling over her shoulder: 'Carry the torch, Rebecca. Carry the torch!'

Rebecca never saw her again for she grew frail soon after that and increasingly eccentric – but she never forgot her.

Silent Eye Productions Ltd had not finished filming, after all. Not quite. Rebecca discovered this by accident, when she cycled down to the Trebizon Bay Hotel in jeans, just before three, to sort out her parents' room booking.

At first, seeing the white van parked outside, she assumed they'd succumbed to the idea of having lunch after all, here at the hotel, and had been taking a long time over it, before booking out. Although that didn't quite square with Elf's intelligence that they were in a tearing rush.

It was only after Rebecca had seen the hotel receptionist (and discovered that her parents were safely booked into the hotel but the confirmation had been sent in error to the London address) that she noticed the sign, just as she was leaving.

It stood at the entrance to a cordoned-off side corridor that led from the hotel's main foyer and said:

NO ENTRY. SILENCE PLEASE. FILMING IN PROGRESS.

Peering down the corridor she saw double glass doors at the end, probably leading into the lounge, thickly curtained. The curtains had been pulled across the glass doors but they didn't quite meet in the middle, so a thin shaft of bright light shone out through the gap, casting a torch-like beam down the dark corridor.

'I wonder what they're filming *here* for?' wondered Rebecca.

She turned to go then, glancing round the deserted foyer, she suddenly turned back. On impulse, she ducked under the cordon and tiptoed down the forbidden corridor, her footsteps silent on the thick pile carpet. Holding her breath, she squinted through the gap in the curtains.

The scene in the hotel lounge was lit up in front of her eyes, like a brilliant tableau. She stared at it, mesmerised for a few seconds.

Both cameras were whirring. An interview was being filmed. The interviewer was Mark

Coughlin, neatly groomed in his dark suit, smiling ingratiatingly and holding out a microphone with a trailing lead that led back to the film unit's sound recording equipment.

The person being interviewed was seated opposite him – a rather stout, bristling sort of a woman, her face turning this way and that towards the cameras. She was wearing what appeared to be her best dress, all frills and flounces, and her hair from the back looked newly set and stiff with lacquer. Rebecca recognised her somehow as being somebody local, somebody connected with the town.

Miss Angel was standing behind the cameras, making little hand signals, creating the curious impression that she was in charge of the whole proceedings. She seemed to be signalling to the woman to keep her head still, just to look straight at the interviewer.

The woman in the chair was droning on in a high-pitched, rather indignant-sounding tone. It seemed to be a monologue but Rebecca couldn't catch any of the words.

Then, getting the message at last, she turned full face to Mark Coughlin. The double chin was quivering, the plump features stained a happy, self-righteous crimson.

Rebecca recoiled, shocked.

It was Mrs Tarkus.

She seemed to be having a field day.

Heart thumping, Rebecca slipped away, ducked under the cordon again and then raced out of the hotel, no longer caring if the receptionist saw her or not. Outside, she leapt on her bike.

All the way up the hill, panting and puffing, turning the pedals as fast as they'd go, the alarm bells were ringing in Rebecca's head.

'Mrs Tarkus! What on earth are they putting

HER in the film for? She hates Trebizon! She's always complaining! She can probably recite off by heart every bit of trouble there's ever been, going back the last twenty years!'

What were they putting HER in the film for?

What kind of film was this going to be ANYWAY?

She turned in the school gates, was soon bumping rapidly along the drive, staring at the main building in the distance. The mellow stone was bathed in summer sunshine. The parkland all around, dotted with old oaks in full leaf at last, was at its most breathtakingly beautiful.

Then Miss Welbeck's words, spoken near the beginning of term, came echoing back, like a cold, chilly whisper.

It can take a hundred years to build up a fine reputation for a school. It can be destroyed almost overnight.

Rebecca turned the handlebars and plunged into the shrubbery, pedalling down the path that was a shortcut to Court House.

TWELVE
Action Committee

'They're making a *horrible* film about Trebizon!' gasped Rebecca, bursting into the big room. She fell on to the nearest bed, lying on her back and gulping to get her breath back after the cycle ride. 'It's going to be one of those "exposé" films! Everything rowdy here – no discipline – parents wasting their money – all that sort of thing! No wonder TV want to take it!'

'Whaa – at?'

Tish switched off her hair dryer. Sue rubbed her nose. Mara's eyebrows shot up. Elf's cheeks started to bulge. And Margot simply said: 'Rebecca, you look as though you need a nice glass of water!' and raced off to the kitchen to get one.

'What's happened, Rebeck?' asked Tish.

'Oh, thank goodness you're all here,' gulped Rebecca, sitting up and looking round. Even as she said it she remembered it was almost time for Tish to go to her big athletics meeting and the others were here to see her off. 'It's going to be a *nasty* film. I know it, I know it, I know it. Oh, *thanks*, Margot.'

She took the glass of water, sipped it gratefully, and with them all gathered round her she told them about Mrs Tarkus.

'Oh, *no*,' groaned Tish.

'Maybe – maybe they just want to get, you know, a sort of balanced picture?' suggested Elf feebly, but without conviction.

'Some hopes!' said Sue. Her face had gone ashen.

'If they'd wanted that, they'd have had Miss Welbeck or somebody there to answer Mrs Tarkus's complaints!' pointed out Rebecca. She was quite positive. Everything added up now. 'For a start, why didn't they film lessons and people working hard, instead of people in the sea all the time, like a holiday camp –?'

'Me surfing,' said Margot, looking alarmed. 'They kept filming me surfing all the time.'

'And you running, Tish,' said Sue, pointedly. 'In Mulberry Cove, remember?'

Tish had gone silent. Susan looked at Rebecca, appalled, and Rebecca nodded her head. She'd thought of it, too. It was almost the first thing she'd thought of.

'They must have *known*. I don't know how, but they knew before they came! About our spending the night on the island.'

'They were taking some shots of the island,' said Tish, very slowly. 'That's what they were doing in the cove, early Monday morning! What else? I never even thought! Why else come to the cove? They wanted to get the island. It was almost the first thing they filmed! And then I appeared on the scene, jogging along in my tracksuit – just like a re-run of the actual event. What a bonus for them!' Tish ran her fingers through her black curls, still very damp after washing her hair under the shower. She, too, was looking appalled now. 'Grief!'

'Oh, they were probably expecting you,' said Rebecca. 'They probably had that all planned, as well.'

'Action committee!' exclaimed Mara, eyes bright and angry. 'We must be the action committee again! You must think of something, Tish!'

'How can I?' wailed Tish. She was still in her

dressing gown. 'Angela Hessel's coming for me in a few minutes!'

The former Olympic medallist was driving Tish to the West of England athletics meeting. She wanted them to be there before six o'clock and the drive would take nearly two hours.

'I know *something* we can do,' said Sue, suddenly. 'We can find out for sure if we're right. If it's the sort of thing we think, there's somebody else they'll have filmed. Isn't there –?'

'Holly Thomas!' exclaimed Rebecca.

'Quick, Sue, go and find Holly,' said Tish urgently, but Sue was already moving towards the door.

'Borrow my bike!' said Rebecca. 'It's by the front porch. But wait a sec, let's think where she'll be –'

Elf looked at her watch and said with some prescience:

'Gone half past three. She'll be watching the gym display. She thinks Lucy Hubbard's wonderful.'

'And while you're getting Holly I'll try and think about Miss Angel!' shouted Tish, and Sue disappeared through the door.

Miss Angel!

Rebecca had almost forgotten about *her*.

'You'd better go and get dressed,' she told Tish. 'But try and remember if you really *have* seen her somewhere before. Elf – you try and draw her face.'

Elf was quite good at faces. But –

'I only saw her once,' she said unhappily. 'She didn't come into school much, did she? I just saw her Wednesday when I was swimming. But I'll try.'

While Tish hurried off to the bathroom with her clothes, Mara found paper and pencil and they gathered round Elf, hopefully, as she tried to sketch the young woman's face.

'Oh, it's no use,' exclaimed the plump girl in frustration, giving up at the third attempt. 'Lots of blonde hair ... the dark glasses ... that's all I remember.'

Tish came back dressed in athletics shorts, found her tracksuit and running shoes and packed her sports bag. She looked worried and tense.

'I'll have to go soon,' she said. 'I've been thinking and thinking about Miss Angel. There *was* something familiar about her and yet there *wasn't*. I can't quite describe it. Maybe if I could see her just once more ... but no chance of that now, is there?'

Margot shrugged her shoulders, getting impatient.

'What's the point anyway? She wasn't anybody important. I saw her a few times, but I never took any notice of her. Why does it matter, Tish? We've got to try and find some way of getting the film stopped, haven't we?'

'We've got to know a bit more about it first,' said Tish stubbornly. 'There was something creepy about Miss Angel. You felt it, too, didn't you, Rebeck –?'

Rebecca nodded.

'And why did they pick on *Trebizon* to pull to pieces?' persisted Tish. 'And assuming they knew about Mulberry Island, *how* did they know? And how did they know to interview Mrs Tarkus and that she's a gas-bag and scandal-monger?'

'Well, perhaps the film director comes from round here?' suggested Margot. 'I mean, he was the one in charge of everything –'

'No!' said Rebecca suddenly.

'Well perhaps he's got friends down here then,' said Margot.

'I don't mean that, Margot. I mean I'm not sure he was the one in charge! I got the most peculiar feeling, when I was down at the hotel just now ... I've only just remembered.'

She explained the odd feeling she'd had, that

Miss Angel was really the boss. The others listened with interest.

'So it's back to Miss Angel again,' said Tish, in some triumph.

'She didn't look quite real, did she?' commented Margot. She was getting more curious about her now. 'She looked very dressed up all the time.'

'Angel,' mused Mara. 'In Greek, the name is common. In England less common? But it is also slang? What does it mean?'

Rebecca gasped.

A person in charge called – *angel*. How odd!

'Clever Mara!' she exclaimed. Mara having a foreigner's view of the English language could see that word with a fresh eye, was questioning something that the rest of them hadn't given any thought to. The word *angel*.

'What does it mean in slang, though?' repeated Mara.

'Isn't it something to do with show business?' hazarded Tish, looking interested.

'An "angel" puts up the money!' said Rebecca. 'The rich backer! The person who puts up the cash needed to stage a play! But why just a play? Why not a film?'

They all looked at Rebecca in admiration. The amount of useless information she stored in her brain! No wonder she usually beat them at Trivial Pursuits!

'Of course, it could be coincidence –' added Rebecca.

'Some coincidence!' exclaimed Tish. 'No, I don't think so. Miss Angel, whoever she *really* is, must have a sense of humour.' She started to pace up and down the room, glanced at her watch, then slapped the side of her head again and again. 'I feel we're edging forward. I feel there's a clue here. Why should someone use a phoney name, unless they're dishonest or something?'

'Just think,' said Elf excitedly, 'if Miss Angel were a crook, then Miss Welbeck might be able to get the film stopped –'

'Stop babbling, Elf,' Tish said despairingly, still pacing up and down. 'My lift will be here any minute. Can't you see I'm trying to *think* –'

But she got no further.

The door burst open and Sue walked in, propelling somebody in front of her. It was Holly Thomas, snuffling, her cheeks tear-stained.

'Ssh, Holly. Stop crying,' Sue said gently. She

carefully closed the door. 'Just tell the others what you've told me. And after that we'll think what to do next.' She looked at Rebecca and added heavily: 'I'm afraid we guessed right. Holly's in the film as well. In fact, she's got what you might call a starring role.'

Tearfully Justin's little sister explained.

It had all been done secretly. 'We want to put you in the film, Holly!' Miss Angel had told her. 'You'll be a TV star, then! You've got just the right

colouring, you know. You'll be very photogenic.'
They'd persuaded her to come down to Mulberry
Cove and they'd filmed her standing by the shore,
pointing to the island. Then they'd asked her to
explain into the microphone how Tish Anderson
had taken them all for a run there, and about the
funny tide, and what an adventure they'd had –
and to be sure to look straight at the camera while
talking.

Afterwards they'd made her swear to keep the
whole thing secret because otherwise the rest of the
First Years would be jealous, wouldn't they? And
they'd want to be in the film, too, but they hadn't
had an exciting adventure, had they? Much better to
say nothing and let it be a surprise.

This had taken place quite early in the week
and Holly had found it all very heady. She'd badly
wanted to be in the film and had persuaded herself
that as she'd been punished at the time and it was
all a long time ago now, nobody would really mind.
She'd hugged the secret to herself ever since. But
gradually her euphoria at the idea of seeing herself
on television had worn off. A niggling feeling of
guilt and anxiety began to take over. What would
Miss Welbeck say? What would Tish and Sue and

Rebecca say? What would Della and Justy say? Justy hadn't even liked her writing about it in The *J.J.*, had he?

So when confronted by Sue, Holly had confessed at once.

'Justy's going to like this *even less*,' Sue had told her through gritted teeth. 'You fool, Holly.'

Tish was even more furious.

'You stupid idiot!' she raged now. 'And I *didn't* take you to the island – you followed us there. This is going to be an exposé type of film – trying to show everyone this is a real dump, or something. It could ruin Trebizon! And you've played right into their hands!'

Holly started to weep again.

'Shut up!' snapped Tish.

'By the way, Angela Hessel's arrived,' said Sue then. 'She's sitting outside in the car. I'm supposed to send you straight down to her.'

Miserably Tish walked across to her bed and picked up her sports bag.

'I'd better go then, hadn't I?' she said dully. She came back and put an arm round Holly's shoulders. 'Sorry I lost my temper. They just made use of you, that's all. It was despicable.' She gazed round at the others. 'What's to do about this film then? Is there any way it can be stopped? I don't suppose there is, really?'

'The only thing we *can* do,' began Rebecca, slowly, 'is report everything we've found out. Miss Welbeck ought to be told. Oughtn't she? It's awful having to admit defeat, but she's really got to know, hasn't she?' Rebecca pulled a wry face. 'And to think it's Commem.'

But everyone agreed there was no other option.

They all trooped downstairs again. Angela Hessel was sitting outside in the car, looking impatient. Tish's face was troubled as everyone wished her luck, by the front porch.

'I'll need it,' she said. She turned to Rebecca and Sue. 'I don't feel much like running tonight,' she said. 'And I wish I'd never thought of going running to the island that time, either. It's led to nothing but bad luck. First for you, Sue ... and now this.'

She was trying to apologise.

Rebecca felt very sad as she watched her get into the waiting car. She'd been training for this race all term, but she wouldn't have her heart in it now, not with this cloud hanging over her. Poor Tish!

The car scrunched away over the gravel.

'Perhaps Miss Welbeck will be able to do something?' said Holly hopefully.

'What?' said Sue. 'What *can* she do?'

'Fine action committee we've turned out to be,' lamented Mara.

THIRTEEN
The Final Clue

'I don't see what we *can* do, George!' said Miss Welbeck, in despair. 'The birds have flown. Half-way back to London now, no doubt, with the film in the can.'

'It's outrageous,' said Colonel Peters, a faint purplish tinge to his cheeks. It was beginning to hit home now, very hard. 'It's quite the most outrageous thing I've ever come across.'

Rebecca and Co. had sent Holly packing, with sealed lips, then lost no time in reporting the facts to Mrs Barrington – who in turn had prised Miss Welbeck away from the party of visitors she was showing round the rose garden, looking at her most summery in a linen dress and a wide-brimmed straw hat and long white fishnet gloves. Leaving Miss Gates to take charge, the Principal had hurried across to her big study in the main building accompanied by Colonel Peters. They'd straight away telephoned the Trebizon Bay Hotel, in the faint hope that Mark Coughlin would agree to see them to discuss the whole matter in a civilised way.

But the film company had left for London.

'They wouldn't have agreed to see us anyway,' sighed Miss Welbeck. 'People like that *aren't* civilised. They've sold the idea to television and they've got what they came to get. Nothing will deflect them now!'

'We've been completely hoodwinked!' fumed Colonel Peters. 'We've got to stop this programme going out next month. Can we get an injunction?'

'Probably not,' said the Principal calmly. 'They'll be careful to put in the film only what's strictly speaking true or, in the case of Mrs Tarkus, what they would describe merely as legitimate expression of local opinion. We *have* had our problems over the years, what school hasn't? There was the shoplifting episode with the Dawson girl, the expulsion of Elizabeth Exton – famous father, colourful stuff, I expect they've managed to dredge *that* one up! – and those wretched parties last summer. There's also the fact that we allow the older girls to mix freely with the Garth boys. We believe that to be right, but it's controversial. Above all, we have the sea here – with all its joys and just occasionally, its dangers, if rules are broken. It's the fact that they've got hold of the Mulberry Island incident that worries me most of all.'

'We must try and stop them!' said the colonel, with renewed vigour. 'A sensationalised and melodramatic picture of life here will set all the parents buzzing with alarm. One film obviously can't destroy Trebizon, but it could put you under pressure to run a tighter ship –'

'This is a tolerably well-run school. I don't think I'd be prepared to change it. I'd have to be replaced, George.'

'Come, Madeleine. Let's think what to do. We must think about legal action, you know.'

'I believe Silver & Silver will advise us against it,' said Miss Welbeck. Silver & Silver were the school's solicitors. 'Even if we won, the publicity would do so much harm! It would cause parents at least as much anxiety as this silly little film!' She shook her head. 'Either way, we can't win.'

There was a heavy silence.

'I'm still amazed that a reputable company could be so downright dishonest about their real intentions!' said the colonel. He walked across to the window and stared out over the parkland. 'You checked up on them carefully. Their record's good. They've produced excellent documentary films in the past – won prizes.'

'Yes. It's very, very puzzling. Unless they're under new management. Do you know the girls have some fanciful idea that Miss Angel is a pseudonym?'

'That sounds like nonsense,' smiled the colonel briefly. 'But there could have been some changes at the top. They could have been bought up, but kept the same name and the goodwill.'

Miss Welbeck sighed. 'I'll make an appointment to see Silver & Silver first thing on Monday morning. They'll advise us.'

Colonel Peters nodded, then walked over to the door, held it open for her and made a slight bow.

'Come. The others will be wondering where we are. It's Commemoration Day. We must rejoin the celebrations.'

'Yes,' said Miss Welbeck. Today was the high point of the school year. The weather, though not quite as beautiful as last year, was being kind. It had all seemed a great success – until now.

'I don't feel there's much to celebrate, do you?' she said bitterly, as they descended the main staircase together.

Halfway down, Miss Welbeck suddenly stopped and looked back over her shoulder.

'What's wrong, Madeleine? Left something behind?'

'That sounds like the phone ringing in my study. Should I answer it?'

'Must you?' he smiled.

The Principal hesitated for a moment, undecided. Then –

'Wait here, George. I'd better go and see who it is.'

Rebecca and Co. didn't feel there was much to celebrate, either. Instead of being out in the sunshine enjoying the activities, they moped about in the empty Common Room on the ground floor of Court House, endlessly discussing what had happened.

Through the window they could see a large white Ford car parked in the front. A chauffeur was stacking the boot with luggage. Margaret Exton was leaving Trebizon today, forever, having taken her final exam. Even that thought didn't cheer them up.

They weren't even looking forward to tonight's Commem Ball that much. They hadn't talked about their dresses all afternoon – or even ironed them yet. The shadow of the day's events cast a blight over everything. Rebecca was convinced that Tish would do badly in her race, too.

'I wonder what Robbie's going to make of all this?' she murmured to Sue.

'Justin's going to be shattered, I just know he is,' said Sue.

Suddenly came the sound of hurrying footsteps and the door burst open. Mrs Barrington stood there, cheeks flushed, puffing slightly.

'Quick! Phone! In the house. Tish wants to talk to you. You, Margot. And Rebecca, I think. You'd all better come –'

They leapt to their feet in surprise and surged out of the Common Room in Mrs Barry's wake. At a fast pace the House Mistress led them through the door that communicated with her private wing.

'What's Tish ringing for?' exclaimed Rebecca. 'She's supposed to be on her way to the race.'

'She is!' retorted Mrs Barry over her shoulder. 'She's halfway there. They've stopped by a public phone box – this is a reverse charge call. It's important. She's just told me something very interesting, but I want it confirmed.'

They all dashed through into the Barringtons' large study, where the phone was off the hook. Rebecca tried to get to the phone first but Margot beat her to it.

'Tish?'

'Margot!' Tish's voice was trembling a little. 'Listen, you saw her more than any of us. Miss Angel, I mean. Tell me if you think what I think –'

There was a moment's silence in the room while Margot closed her eyes tight, then opened them again, then squealed:

'Yes! Yes, yes, yes!'

She handed over the phone to Rebecca. 'Hurry! *You* talk to her!'

'What's going on?' wailed Sue.

'Listen Rebeck,' crackled Tish's voice, 'I know who Miss Angel is now. The final clue was in the name, all the time. Clever you! Knowing it meant a rich backer and so on! All the time in the car I've been thinking, who do I know who's rich? Rich enough to finance a whole film production? Who have I *ever* known who's really rich –?'

'Tish, get *on* with it –' cried Rebecca. 'Who then? Who?'

'Elizabeth Exton!'

'*No!*' Rebecca nearly dropped the phone.

'It's her, I tell you. She's Miss Angel.'

'But she didn't have blonde hair!'

'Dyed, I expect. Or even a wig. It's her. I *know* it is!'

Margot was looking fervent in the background, whispering to the others. 'It's Elizabeth Exton, I tell you. Once you know, you can just shut your eyes and *see* it.'

Susan, Mara and Elf looked thunderstruck. And Rebecca, just as they were, was trying to visualise Miss Angel with straight black hair. No fluorescent make-up. No dark glasses. Nearly three years younger. And wearing the clothes of a member of the Upper Sixth at Trebizon. Because that would have been her last sight of Elizabeth Exton, the exalted and rather remote senior girl that they'd tangled with (especially Tish) in Rebecca's very first term at Trebizon. With a slight shiver of recognition, she remembered the face in the car park at Exonford.

'The eyes!' she said suddenly. 'You're right, Tish. How amazingly clever of you.'

Mrs Barry had been listening to all this with considerable interest.

'Good luck with the race, Tish!' said Rebecca quickly, just before Mrs Barry took the phone from her.

'We've got them now, haven't we, Rebeck!' Tish was saying happily. 'Won't they just look sick when this comes out –'

'Tish?' said Mrs Barry. 'It's me again. Look, I want you to hang on a minute. With luck, we'll catch Miss Welbeck. I know where she's gone. I'm going to try and transfer the call. I think it's important you speak to her. Okay? Hold the line.'

The Principal picked up the phone on the eighth ring. 'Yes?'

'It's Joan Barrington here, Miss Welbeck. I've got Tish Anderson on the line. She's ringing from a call box, on her way to the West of England meeting. It's a reverse charge call, so she won't run out of money. May I transfer her?'

'Certainly,' said the Principal, puzzled. After a few clicks: 'Well, Ishbel. What's the trouble exactly?'

A moment later she sank down on to her chair, feeling a little weak at the knees. 'Will you repeat that, Ishbel?'

Miss Angel – Elizabeth Exton!

Tish was racing on, like an express train, but the Principal was no longer listening.

She was remembering all sorts of things. The drama of Elizabeth's dishonest behaviour, almost three years ago, exposed by young Tish Anderson!

Rebecca Mason had helped, too, hadn't she? And then, this term, the awkward business of Margaret Exton having to leave, too. The bitter interview with the father. Most unpleasant. Not something the mind dwelled upon.

Although the Principal couldn't recollect Miss Angel's face (had she even met her?) she never felt a moment's doubt.

'I'm sure you and your friends are right, Ishbel. Quite sure. It explains all.'

And she could already see in her mind's eye the kind of letter that Silver & Silver would be instructed to dispatch to *Silent Eye Productions Ltd*, after the weekend:

> ... *should the film go ahead on the lines envisaged, both the media and the Independent Broadcasting Authority will be informed of your actions in sending a disgraced former pupil (who had been expelled for dishonesty) back to her old school under an assumed name, bent solely on an act of revenge . . .*

'Will the film be stopped now, Miss Welbeck?' Tish was asking eagerly.

'Oh, yes, Ishbel,' the Principal replied confidently.

'It will be stopped dead in its tracks.'

'Elizabeth always wanted to be a journalist, didn't she, Miss Welbeck? Do you think her father bought her the film company because that was the only way she could get into that sort of field?'

'I'm sure he did, Ishbel,' replied the Principal.

'And then Margaret must have told her about the Mulberry Island business and she thought she'd found a really good story?'

'Presumably.' 'And the chance to get her revenge,' thought Miss Welbeck. Her hands went slightly clammy. '*And she very nearly got away with it!*'

'Ishbel, you'll be late for your race meeting if you don't go,' she said kindly. 'You have been extremely bright. I'm very pleased with you.'

'No, it's Rebecca Mason who's been bright, Miss Welbeck!' insisted Tish. 'She knew what "angel" meant in slang. You know – the person who puts up the money, that's what it means!'

'So it does!'

Miss Welbeck replaced the receiver and laughed to herself in surprise. Well done, Rebecca! And how stupid of Elizabeth Exton, to turn her pseudonym into a little joke. That was her one fatal mistake, it seemed. Colonel Peters looked into the room.

'Hallo, Madeleine, you look more cheerful suddenly.'

'I feel it!' she replied, rising to her feet and walking across to him. 'But I'm afraid school as a whole will be very disappointed when they hear the sad news next week.'

'Oh?'

'There's to be no television film about Trebizon after all.'

<u>FOURTEEN</u>
A Famous Term

The word went round much sooner than that. It was one of the main talking points at the Commem Ball! The news had spread like wildfire.

Rebecca and her friends, and Robbie and the other boys, just couldn't keep quiet about it. It had all been so extraordinary. As they passed each other on the dance floor, they kept laughing and making jokes – 'Whoops, look out! There's a camera hidden behind the curtains!' – 'That man in the band looks a bit suspicious. I think he's in disguise!' – 'What's he holding a mike for? Look out, Rebecca! Be careful what you say to Robbie!'

They laughed until the tears ran down their cheeks, weak with relief that such an awful crisis had been averted so narrowly, and of course other people soon got wind of the story and kept rushing up to ask if it was all really true.

It was amazing, wasn't it!

At one stage during the evening a group of indignant Sixth Formers went off to try and find Margaret Exton, but of course she'd gone.

Miss Welbeck had let her go only too readily.

'No, I don't think I want to interview her, Barry,' she'd told the House Mistress when asked, shortly after Tish's phone call. 'I don't know to what extent Margaret was a party to all this and really I'm past caring. Let her go. I've seen enough of the Exton family to last me a lifetime.'

Rebecca savoured every moment of that evening. After all the tension, the relief of the narrow escape heightened her enjoyment one-hundredfold.

Robbie was wearing a dinner suit! He'd bought it secondhand in the Save the Children shop in the town, an old-fashioned one made by a tailor, with rounded-off satin lapels, silk-lined jacket and waistcoat – but a perfect fit. He'd found it four weeks earlier and picked up a black bow tie and white dress shirt to go with it, from the Oxfam shop. 'The whole lot came to less than fifteen pounds,' he told Rebecca. As they took the floor together for the first dance, she thought he'd never looked more handsome.

He told her ruefully that another boy had won the tennis cup at Garth this year. 'I'm completely out of practice,' he confessed.

He'd been studying so hard; he was taking this Oxbridge business very seriously.

He thought Rebecca was wearing a new outfit, too, and admired it. She wasn't! It was the one she'd worn last year: the lovely shimmering blue dress with fringes that Mara's Aunty Papademas had bought her, the one that had caused a lot of trouble at the time. But now she'd discarded the matching blue stole and saved up to buy a dramatic black one layered with white fringes that matched the fringes on the dress. 'You're not very observant, Robbie!' she teased him.

Mara looked lovely, of course. And so did Susan. Really lovely! Like Joss, she'd be sixteen in September. She hadn't wanted to borrow a dress after all, just settling for the one she usually wore when she played at concerts. Rebecca reflected that apart from having an enviable figure, Sue had a new-found poise tonight, making that dress look much more special than it really was, making heads turn whenever she and Justin took to the dance floor.

They all ate supper together, outside in the quadrangle gardens. Standing out there with Robbie and her friends, as dusk fell, Rebecca suddenly felt almost overwhelmed by the sight of the lights flickering on in the buildings all around them while at just the same time the delicate sweetness of the night-scented stocks began to pervade the air. She loved Trebizon! She loved these gardens!

To complete her happiness, Angela Hessel's car arrived back just as the Ball had ended. They were all drifting outside to see the boys on to their coach, when the Nissan pulled up right beside the coach and Tish tumbled out.

She'd had a wonderful race.

Against older and much more experienced distance runners she'd come in fifth!

'A remarkable triumph,' Angela Hessel explained to them, in delight. 'She's done wonders!'

'That's not the only way she's done wonders!' exclaimed Laura Wilkins, breaking away from Mike Brown to join the headlong rush towards Tish. Like almost everyone else, Laura knew the whole story by now. 'Thank goodness you recognised Elizabeth Exton, Tish. Brilliant!'

Everybody wanted to shake her hand and pat her on the back. But at last Robbie and Rebecca pulled her clear and managed to get her to themselves.

'Congratulations, Tish,' said Rebecca.

'Clever girl,' added Robbie.

They both kissed her on the cheek.

'I'm starving,' said Tish. 'Is there any food left?'

They laughed as Robbie produced some sausage rolls from the pocket of his dinner jacket saying, 'I'd saved these for the coach. Here, you have them!' and

Tish responded, 'Oh, is the coach hungry then?'

Sue and Justin had been amongst the very first to congratulate Tish, but there was no sign of them now.

And when Mr Slade started counting the boys on to the coach, Justin was still missing. 'We'll find him, sir!' said Robbie.

The threesome walked through to quadrangle gardens at the back, then halted.

At the far end of the terrace, Justin and Sue stood face to face, just gazing at one another wordlessly, with enraptured expressions. They appeared to have lost any sense of time.

'Oh, doesn't Sue look lovely?' whispered Rebecca. 'She looks so happy now!'

'So does Justy,' added Robbie, feeling pleased.

Tish just grinned and said to them, wryly:

'I suppose it was all worth it?'

Rebecca hesitated for a moment, then raised a smile.

'Oh, Tish, don't be so unromantic. Of course it was worth it.'

Robbie put three fingers to his lips and let forth a piercing whistle. The pair at the other end of the terrace gave a little start, as though roused from a dream. And then Robbie cupped his hands round his mouth and shouted:

'Coach, Justy!'

He then took Rebecca's hand in his and they started to make their way back. 'Come and see me off, Rebeck.' Tish broke away from them, hands in the pockets of her track top.

'See you back at Court, Rebecca,' she said. 'I'll put the kettle on.' Over her shoulder, she gave Justin and Sue a final glance. They still seemed very, very reluctant to make a move. 'If Justy hangs about much longer,' she said, with another grin, 'he'll find the coach has turned back into a pumpkin, won't he?'

The surmise that Freddie Exton now owned *Silent Eye Productions Ltd* had been correct. It wasn't public knowledge because he'd bought it through a holding company, the previous summer. He'd made staff changes, put Elizabeth on the board and given her a key role there, with the chance to try her hand at making films. With her lack of qualifications and bad school record, it was the only way he could get her started in the kind of work she wanted to do.

Again, a correct surmise.

Elizabeth, known these days more racily as Libby, had had some crackpot ideas for films which had come to nothing, so that her father had been losing patience with her. But Margaret's account of what Tish Anderson had got away with at Trebizon, at the beginning of the term (which she'd mentioned to the family rather bitterly at half-term), had given Elizabeth the idea of the Trebizon film.

She'd always sworn to get her revenge on Tish if ever the chance presented itself, and now the time had come. Even better, at the same time she could get her revenge on Trebizon in general. Margaret was leaving anyway! She would settle her own score and settle the score for Margaret at the same time.

The idea was suggested to a television company in much more demure terms, of course, under the working title *Trebizon Observed* – and had immediately been accepted.

So both Tish and Miss Welbeck had been correct in all the things they'd surmised, with one exception.

Miss Welbeck had averred that there could be no television film about Trebizon now.

She was wrong.

'You ninny!' Freddie Exton had raged at his daughter, the day after the letter from Silver &

Silver arrived. 'Letting yourself be recognised! Why didn't you keep out of the way? I warned you to be careful! The company's been losing money for six months now and we could have recouped it all with this film. We'd made a sale to TV. It was going to be networked!'

'I think we can *still* make a sale, sir,' butted in Nik Coster, the film's producer. 'In fact I'm *sure* we can.'

He could see that Freddie Exton was in a dangerous mood: a mood to wind up the company. It had been a lucky break for Nik, meeting Elizabeth at her twenty-first birthday party and landing this job. He wasn't going to see his career wrecked without putting up a fight. And besides . . .

He'd been looking at the rushes of the film and having a long discussion with the videotape editor.

'We could cut out all the scandal and still have a great film!' he insisted, before anyone could stop him. 'We've got some marvellous sequences. Beautiful colour effects! There's this black girl – she's a brilliant surfer ... We've got a great chunk of the founder's day service. Mark took it just to use up the rest of the film, but it's rather lovely. Very English. Best of all, sir, there's this tennis match. Two gorgeous girls, brilliant tennis, what more could TV want? The school would pass a film like that. They couldn't possibly object . . .'

'You rat, Nik!' hissed Libby Exton, finding her voice at last.

But Freddie Exton was looking extremely interested. He was a businessman and a hard-headed one. He didn't like losing money. He hated it. He didn't like any of his companies to fail . . .

'You let them make a nice film about Trebizon and I resign, Daddy!'

He didn't like being told what to do, either.

'You'd better resign then,' he said to his daughter, a cold little glitter in his eye. Then, turning straight to his film producer: 'Okay, Nik. Go ahead. Get the film together. Show it to the school solicitors and get their agreement in writing. And make it good.'

'Leave it to me, sir,' said Nik Coster, mopping his brow in relief.

Freddie Exton hurried from the building, into his chauffeur-driven car and on to the next company meeting, feeling in a much better mood now.

It looked as though *Silent Eye* might be moving up into profit at last.

So that was how the Trebizon film appeared on television after all. The controversial items were completely expunged. The interview with Mrs Tarkus, in its entirety, ended up on the cutting room floor. She was deeply disappointed.

The reviewers thought it was a stunning film and everyone agreed that the tennis sequences, showing in full the last four games between Rebecca and Joss in the final of the county closed, made a brilliant climax.

It became a famous match, in the literal sense of the word.

It had been a famous term!

In the week that followed Commem, all sorts of important things happened.

Rebecca's summer ranking came through from the LTA – she'd moved up to fortieth place in her age group! And because of the results she'd had since the deadline for the computer, her true position was obviously higher still.

The day after her ranking arrived, she sent in her application form for the British Junior Grasscourt Championships at Eastbourne and crossed her fingers.

Oddly enough, Robbie's Oxford Entrance Form went off on the very same day, with the colleges listed in order of preference – the one he'd been to the weekend of Tish's birthday at the top. And so he crossed his fingers, too.

Sue forgot to do her violin practice three afternoons running, quite unheard of, because she was meeting Justin down town for coffee after school.

Tish received an invitation to run in the 1500 metres at an athletics meeting in Birmingham at the end of August.

And summer exams began.

Rebecca regarded them almost as an intrusion upon her life now.

With the dream of getting to Eastbourne this year about to become a reality, she was out on the grass courts early morning, lunch time and late into the evenings, practising her strokes with anybody and everybody willing to spare the time. Joss turned out a great deal and Robbie came over from Garth College at least twice. The staff helped, too, especially Miss Darling. ('The Dread's being a darling,' as Tish put it.) And at other times, when the whole world seemed to be swotting, Rebecca was swatting the tennis ball instead – creeping out and swatting it against the end wall of Norris House, where she couldn't disturb anyone and there weren't any windows to break.

So Rebecca, languages and English literature apart, did badly in her end-of-year exams. She failed to reach the pass mark in maths and the science subjects. Even in history she only just scraped through, having spent no time revising the period on which they were being tested.

And when her parents arrived at the end of term and went to meet Miss Welbeck for the long awaited discussion about her future, Rebecca felt distinctly nervous.

She preferred not to think about what might be taking place at that interview and tried to enjoy the little end-of-term party that Fiona Freeman and Jenny Brook-Hayes had organised at Court House, instead.

To her surprise, when her parents emerged from their lengthy session with the Principal, they seemed to be in a good mood. They didn't volunteer any information and they didn't seem to want Rebecca to question them, but they seemed perfectly happy. Slightly jubilant, even, in a secretive sort of way!

Rebecca just gave a huge sigh of relief.

'Everything all right?' asked the others anxiously,

before breaking up time and the parting of the ways. 'Your parents happy?' queried Tish.

'Happy as larks, as far as I can see,' smiled Rebecca.

Even so, travelling back to London by car with them next morning, Rebecca was slightly mystified to note that the air of quiet jubilation still seemed to linger on.

'Well, it's been a good year, hasn't it?' said her father.

'You're coming along nicely at Trebizon, aren't you, Becky?' agreed her mother.

'Is – is Miss Welbeck really pleased with me then?' asked Rebecca, unable to hide her curiosity any longer. 'I mean, she's quite thrilled about Eastbourne, then?'

'Eastbourne?' Her father frowned for a moment, concentrating on the road. He was keeping a lookout for the motor-way signs. 'Oh, yes. She's pleased about that, too, of course.'

Rebecca wondered what else the Principal could possibly be pleased about. She could hardly be pleased about her exam results. And as Rebecca certainly didn't want to draw attention to *those* unnecessarily she decided to say no more. Instead, she snuggled back comfortably in the speeding car and watched the hedges rush by.

'Maybe it's because of the film business?' she thought. 'Who cares! Mum and Dad are happy!'

And so was she.

In two days' time it would be her fifteenth birthday and for once she'd be spending it at home with her parents. They were taking her on a shopping spree as a birthday present this year, to the big London stores!

The long summer holidays stretched ahead, full of promise. Her year in the Fourth at Trebizon lay behind her now. It had been an important year for some of them, in one way or another, with the prospect of even bigger things to come.

And next term they'd all be moving up.

For 'the six', that meant literally moving up – to the top floor of Court House. It was good up there. You were given your own cubicle with bed and desk, with space on the partition walls for pictures and posters of your choice and each cubicle had its own little window. You could see right across to main school from those dormer windows and if you were lucky, according to Moyra Milton, you'd get birds nesting up there in the eaves, just above.

'*Moving up!*' thought Rebecca, with pleasure.

Into the Fifth. The year of her GCSE exams, perhaps the most important year of all . . .

Next year was going to be different. She'd make a fresh start. Turn over a new leaf. Do all her GCSE assignments brilliantly. Then the exams! She'd slog and slog and slog! She really would.

Next year. In the Fifth.